Evan, now have a
you bona fide author
in the family; I
would pay that you
enjoy reading as much
as he does.
Love,
Gram

The Flipt family welcomes
you as a friend.

Dean

Touch the Moon

Wills W. Black

INFI∞ITY
PUBLISHING

Copyright © 2010 by Dean W. Williams

ISBN 0-7414-5885-3

Printed in the United States of America

This is a work of fiction. Names, characters, places, and incidents either are the product of the author's imagination or are used fictitiously. Any resemblance to actual events or locales or persons, living or dead, is entirely coincidental.

Published March 2010

INFINITY PUBLISHING
1094 New DeHaven Street, Suite 100
West Conshohocken, PA 19428-2713
Toll-free (877) BUY BOOK
Local Phone (610) 941-9999
Fax (610) 941-9959
Info@buybooksontheweb.com
www.buybooksontheweb.com

To Misha, who found her family.
She was always generous and
always grateful.

Contents

CHAPTER 1

INTO THE DRAGON

The two sled teams were poised at the brink of Big Hill. Although they had been here before, they were nervous. The dark emptiness of sky made the stars seem small and the moon like a dish of cloudy ice. The whispery stillness of biting cold made the night seem as if time had stopped. Should they go?

The two teams looked down... and down... and **down,** and what they saw was very scary. Big Hill was steep. Almost straight down. In fact, the world below Big Hill plunged so deep, and stretched so far, all of them knew that the smallest mistake would send them off into dark space from which they might not return.

The midnight moon was nearly full. Its icy silvery light seemed to give objects a brittle metallic look. A nasty little wind crept under their helmets and whispered about icebergs and glaciers. The two teams had never done anything like this before. No wonder they were nervous.

"Teams ready?"

"Team One, r-r-ready," a young, trying-to-be-brave voice said.

"Second team, uh, same th-thing."

The Team One Driver looked through the windshield of his Zebra Racer. He saw mostly black sky. "Anything we should r-remember?" he asked, looking for a little reassurance.

"Yes," the Team One Pusher replied, in a deep voice. "Let us not forget that this is a big adventure. Huge! We, all of us, are embarking on an adventure so important, so inventive..."

"Fred," the Team Two Pusher interrupted, "if we're going to go, let's go. All of you remember two things. One: Watch Out For The Cat! Two: We only go down the Hill a short distance and stop. This is a test. It is NOT a **RACE,** so be careful. Fred, anything more to be careful about?"

"Absolutely, my dear," Fred said solemnly. "Listen up, Teams. Before we begin this historic test ride, I want everyone to look around and see how very different our new Jungle is. Although it is not warm and green like the Jungle from which our parents came, this black and white landscape has its own beauty. Take everything in, Betsy, children."

Though Fred did tend to make long speeches, this was absolutely the right thing to say. The Fliffs were looking at a new world. It was so big and cold and different and distant and strange. Maybe one or two of the Fliffs had to ask themselves if they really should be out here. It was not an easy question to answer.

To the left and the right, far and near, the land and trees had a silvery coating. But where the moonlight could not reach, the shadows were black and empty. The air was like frozen silence. It was a stark and strangely beautiful Jungle, completely unlike the steamy green tangle of leaves and vines from which the Fliff ancestors had come.

The two teams did take it all in, and asked themselves: Yes or No? Go or No Go? Oh, what the heck. It's just a test, right? That's all. Easy. They looked at each other through goggles. Six brave faces. The Team One Driver nodded to the other Driver. A small nod, but that was the message: Now or never. Driver Two nodded back. Now! The sled Pushers paused, took deep breaths, waved bravely to each other, and that was it. They were ready.

So was someone else.

The Pushers slid the Zebra Racers back and forth on the sleds' runners the way they had seen Olympic bobsled racers start. They weren't sure why. Maybe the sleds had to be awakened? Warmed up?

Ha! The Zebra sleds did not need to be awakened or encouraged to go. They were ready, willing, and able to zoom down this hill or any other hill you'd care to put beneath their metal runners. But wait. Maybe the sharp ice crystals could scratch the runners and wear them out? Ha, again. The metal runners, which had been so carefully shaped and sharpened by Fred, were just waiting to bite and turn and slide and fly atop the icy surface.

Two days ago when the Test was being planned, Fred and Betsy decided that they were going to steer the sleds. It would be a risky business, piloting the Zebra sleds in this new, very dangerous Jungle. If mistakes are made, Fred and Betsy thought that it would be better if they made them, rather than the children. However, as they talked it over, they ended up agreeing that Rhoda and Sherman had really proven themselves this winter. Rhoda's work on Moonseeker was brilliant. Sherman's designs had been terrific, too, first on the Elevator, and then the Retriever. Very smart work indeed.

Just as important, Rhoda and Sherman had behaved well. They had done their chores without too much complaining and they had been nice to the little kids. So that was why Fred and Betsy reconsidered the matter and decided to let Rhoda and Sherman do the piloting. Besides, it was only a test run. Not risky at all. They wouldn't be going far. It'll be easy as beet pie. Easy and fun.

But now, outdoors in the new and real world full of unknowns, Fred and Betsy's doubts were as big as the Hill. Well, this was the moment of truth—Go now or go home.

"**Here we go!**" Fred shouted bravely. He began pushing.

"*Fliffs go,*" Betsy said, but more softly. She began pushing, too.

Both Pushers (the right kind) ran and pushed hard. The sleds picked up speed quickly, on the icy crust.

Picked up speed, alright. The two Zebra sleds practically **flew**. In less than twenty feet the sleds were zinging down Big Hill. In ten seconds they were going so fast that details of the moon-washed landscape became blurry. The two Pushers had jumped into the sleds just in time.

"I'M GOING TO TRY THE BRAKES!" Fred yelled. He pulled the brake lever, the hooks began to dig in, and the Zebra lurched wildly from side to side. Sherman quickly corrected the steering. If he hadn't, they would have spun around, flipped, and crashed.

"DON'T USE THE BRAKES!" Sherman yelled to his father.

Fred glanced to his right. The other Zebra had done the same thing. Oh no! But Rhoda also had excellent reflexes and corrected the skid. That was the good news. But now both sleds were plunging down Big Hill at top speed. Fred knew in an instant that they were in big trouble. A test? A short run? No way: They—Could—Not—Stop! They were headed all... the... way... down... BIG HILL.

"HOLD ON!" he heard Betsy yell. The warning came just in time. Side by side, the Zebras whipped U-p-p-p a small hillock, flew off the crest, and sailed into the frigid night air. Everyone's stomach went up and stayed there, suspended and confused... until the Zebras smacked down on hard crust.

Sherman's sled skidded. He straightened it out. Rhoda's sled landed on one set of runners and almost rolled over, but Rhoda steered correctly and the team leaned in the opposite direction. Her Zebra was back on both sets of runners. That was too close for comfort!

The next time they were ready for the Dipsy-Doodle. Both drivers hit the bump with their Zebras flying straight and true. The sleds leapt into the cold night air and then down and down they plunged... **BANG, BANG!** The landings

5

were hard but they didn't tip over. That was the good news.

The bad news was, now the Fliffs were careening down the STEEPEST part of the hill. Wind roared past them and took their breaths away. They were going faster than jet planes. This wasn't Big Hill. It was **SUPER HILL**.

Incredibly, the sleds went even faster. The wind shrieked in their ears and froze their brave faces. Tiny crystals of ice flew off the runners of one sled and made RAT-a-TAT sounds as they hit the other sled's windshield.

Earlier, the sleds had made a tsyk... tsyk... tsyk...cha chattering noise as they zinged over tiny bumps in the crust. At the speed they were going now—easily TWICE as fast as before—the Zebras *flew* across the tops of those bumps. They were going so fast the sleds seemed to be traveling on a cushion of hurricane air... Tsss... ss... ss... sss. The scenery whirred by in a blur... just tiny glimpses of a bump there, a bush, a rock... One false move at this speed and it would be Disasterville!

But the drivers were smart. All Guinea Pigs are smart. The two Drivers knew instinctively how to make small, careful steering corrections to get around dangerous obstacles. They knew that if you panicked and steered too hard, the sled would skid out of control and smash into a tree. Or a rock. These pilots, these two Guinea Pigs: No panic for them.

The danger had not gone away, however. Father poked his head up, to look around Sherman. The hill was leveling out a little bit—at least it didn't seem straight down. Ahead was a small field, with big bushes and more bumps. Bad enough, but the shadows were deeper here and in some places it was impossible to see beyond a certain jump or around a larger bush. It was the UNKNOWN!

Fred thought about the brakes, and why they didn't work right. Of course! Instead of having a brake hook on *each* side of the Zebra, there should have been a double hook in the middle, in back. Too late for that now.

"TRY TO STEER INTO SNOWY SECTIONS," he yelled across to Rhoda, as they flew off a small hump. **"THE SNOW WILL SLOW US DOWN!"**

As Fred was trying to look ahead, suddenly he was overtaken by a <u>huge dark shadow</u>. It was so large it seemed to fill the sky. The moon and the stars disappeared. It felt as if a huge black blanket had been thrown over them. Although he was terrified of what he might see, Fred forced himself to look up. He was sorry he looked.

It was *HORRIBLE!* The thing... it was a thing, a Creature... was enormous. And it was alive and flying and going faster than they were. Fred caught a glimpse of the huge beast. He wanted to shut his eyes. He wanted the earth to open and swallow them up. He knew this was the END.

It was a monstrous ugly winged fire-breathing clawed DRAGON!

Fred shivered and gulped. He blinked hard, and against his own wishes, he looked again. OmiGOSH. The monster flying over their heads was no Creature of the Jungle. It wasn't even from the Earth itself. It had mighty legs and a great long tail and its head was the size of a... of a... DINOSAUR.

Fred's life flashed before him. He was facing the end. He and his family. What kind... How did... *"Spirit of the Cold Jungle, we have done the wrong thing,"* Fred muttered. *"We have made a terrible mistake. We meant no harm but somehow we have awakened a Dragon. This is the end of our little family. And it is all my fault. Punish me, but please, please spare my family."*

A deep sadness fell over Fred. Charlie, their littlest lad, was scrunched down between him and Sherman. Charlie's head was wrapped tightly by his small arms. Sherman's head was ducked down, so he could just see over the cowling. Yes, these two had seen the thing, and so had Team Two.

Fred was sorry they had seen the DRAGON, too. Now they would know what was going to happen. He wished he could confront the Creature alone and trade himself for the others. This was all his fault. Well, not all, not exactly all. Betsy's Ideas about 'Getting Around' and 'Getting up the cage wall' had started these wild adventures, but Fred knew he could have just said No.

The Dragon had flown ahead and as soon as the sky cleared, Fred came to a decision. Because it was his fault, he would make the sacrifice. When they slowed down, he would leap off the Zebra Racer and go talk to the Dragon and ask it to let the others go. If worse came to worse and the monster said NO, Fred would have no choice. He would defend his wonderful family as best he could. Fliff pride gave him some courage.

With his heart pounding, Fred was trying to be brave so he could say Goodbye to his family and confront the dreadful Beast. He would warn them to run and hide while he held the Great Beast off. Maybe they could escape... **Oh no**...

Directly ahead, hulking between two trees, sat the thing. The DRAGON! It was huge, with huge ears and crazy scales and gigantic teeth. Bigger than Audrey II, Frankenstein, and the Rider from Sleepy Hollow. The Zebra sleds were speeding directly to it.

Both Fliff pilots saw the terrible Beast. Sherman, with lightning-fast reflexes, twisted the steering to the left to avoid the hulking monster. There was a small gap at the base of a heavy bush. Sherman shot through and it was OPEN AHEAD.

Fred turned. Team Two had made it through the gap, too.

"HEAD FOR DEEP BRUSH AT THE BOTTOM," he yelled. **"MAYBE WE CAN HIDE."**

The final sprint across the last stretch of open hill seemed to take forever this time. The Zebras were slowing a little bit. Sherman was steering toward a clump of brush that looked pretty thick. Maybe... The Zebras, nose to tail, slashed through the brush, careening off small stumps, skidding around rocks, always trying to get deeper into the bushes.

Oh **NO**! Suddenly they burst *OUT OF THE BRUSH*, into a small clearing. Worse yet, snow had piled in here and the Zebras just slowed, stutter-stepped, and stopped dead. Stopped. In the open. But that wasn't the worst part. Oh no. The world's worst part was right there in front of them. Sitting. Grinning. Ready to... It was the monstrous hulk of the terrible **DRAGON**. Waiting for them. It had known all along that they'd be trapped in here.

Fred pulled his small but strong muscles together and hoped he would be able to defend his family, even a little. He swung his stout but strong little body out of the Zebra racing sled. In what would be his final seconds on Earth, for some strange reason, Fred couldn't help but think back and wonder **HOW** they could have gotten into a pickle like this. A month ago, even a week ago, life had seemed so... so simple. Now, because of Silly Ideas, he and his family were facing... facing... Fred couldn't say it.

Apparently the monster had ideas worth saying, though. It opened its huge mouth, a mouth with gigantic teeth that glinted like knives, and it spoke in a voice that sounded like a cave full of demons:

"WELL, WELL. TWO HOLES IN THE GROUND. WE MEET AGAIN."

Two? Father Fliff's last two thoughts were:

I hope my family escapes, and

How did this happen?

Then he remembered something about *The Wall*, and *Getting... Around*. Did those simple things push us into the Jaws of Disaster? Was it worth... this? Well, Fred, he said to himself, there's no choice in the matter. Do your best, Old Fellow.

CHAPTER 2

A LIVING LADDER

(Or: "How It All Started A Month Ago!")

The Winter had begun very oddly. Some years are like that.

First, Betsy (known to the kids as Mother) had gotten some strange idea about dancing.... No, no, wait. The really odd stuff actually began *before* the Dance Torture Episode. The oddities really had begun with Charlie.

Charlie was the younger lad, and he was way different from his similar-age sister, Oyster. Charlie was quiet and careful. When Charlie got an Idea... (Do you know that Ideas are the favorite brain food of Guinea Pigs? Yes. They are wildly crazy about Ideas!) When Charlie got an Idea he chewed on it, like a cow quietly chews a cud, before he tried it out. Oyster, the youngest Fliff child, was noisy. When she had an Idea, she jumped right into it with both feet. Anyway, early in the winter, Charlie told everyone that he had invented a brand new "Guessing Game."

"Oh, that's nice," someone said, to be polite. Charlie's games were not very interesting. "What are we supposed to guess about?"

"This," Charlie said mysteriously, holding up a reddish-colored shaving. "Guess what kind of wood it is."

"Heart of red cedar," Rhoda answered quickly, and went back to doing her homework.

Charlie stared at her for a minute. "You cheated," he finally said.

At this point, Rhoda could have explained that *anyone* knows what red cedar looks like, but she was busy and didn't feel like arguing with her little brother. So she said, "Yes, I did cheat. I peeked inside your head and the answer was written on your eyelid. Ha ha."

That was the end of the Guessing Game but the start of something much bigger. Much, **much** bigger!

A week after the Guessing Game failure, a Tuesday afternoon after school, Chloe took Betsy out of the cage so they could watch TV together. Later, back in the cage, Betsy was all excited about a program she had seen. "It was so interesting, Fred," she said. "About dancing."

Fred (known to the kids as Father) smiled and said nothing. He had heard the program and knew immediately that he wanted absolutely nothing to do with it. Dancing? I don't think so.

"All of us would **really** enjoy it," she continued. "And I know, I just know, I could even teach **you** to dance, Fred. Especially with that name of yours. What a nice coincidence."

Coincidence? Fred was not going to bite the bait. He had seen programs where energetic humans whirled around the dance floor like leaves in a cyclone. Definitely not his style, all those spins and flings. Sure, if Betsy wanted a slow waltz, he could do that. But the jittery jerky chicken stuff... No, uh unh, sorry, won't do, can't do, don't like, no, sorry...

Well, as it turned out, Fred was right about the 'Can't Do' part but wrong about the 'Won't Do'. For five or ten or maybe a million days the Fliff family tried... tried... to do Betsy's idea of *'Enormously great fun'*—the SQUARE DANCE. It was pure torture.

Betsy's family did try. Really. But, let's face it, Guinea Pigs are not perfectly suited to HOP GOOSEY HOP, LEAP OVER THE WATER BOWL, or a dozen other Square Dance steps too humiliating to mention. Luckily for Fred, the children shared his discomforts. One day, as if caused by magic, the Dancing-Is-Fun Episode ended with a barrage of complaints:
Twisted Knee (Rhoda),
Sprained Knee (Sherman),
Sore Neck (Charlie),
Bent Toenail (Oyster, who had to be different),
and
Sore All Over (Father).

Betsy looked at their faces, which were trying hard to scrunch into painful poses. They were terrible actors but she understood the gentle rebellion. Smiling bravely at the cageful of make-believe medical patients, she declared, "Well, I am so glad you all agree that dancing has been fun. Now it's time to try other funs."

That was the end of dancing. Fliff-type creatures are not made for certain activities and they are not too stubborn to admit it.

But that was *not* the end of Ideas.

More recently, one quiet afternoon, Fred had been thinking about a nice nap. However, a tiny alarm bell told him **'No, don't.'** Fred noticed... no, he *sensed* that something odd was going to happen. Guinea Pigs are like that, you know. Keen observers with keen instincts.

He looked around the cage. Everything seemed normal... No, wait, there it was. Betsy, standing in the corner of the cage, looking up. Was she actually looking up? Or just stretching her graceful neck muscles? Or was it something d-a-n-g-e-r-o-u-s?

Fred's alarm system went on Full Alert. Maybe Betsy was having a notion, an Idea. Hmm... mmm. Fred sat perfectly still except for his dark eyelids, which narrowed to squinty slits as he peered cautiously at Betsy. Observing without being seen. In times of danger Fred Fliff *knew* the Ways of the Jungle and he immediately *behaved* like a Jungle creature: Hear without being noisy, see without being seen, move without... well, move quietly, and so forth.

Ah! Then came the clue he had been waiting for. Betsy said, mostly to herself, "My goodness, isn't this wall tall!" With that, she stood on tip toes and reached as high as she could.

What was she after, Fred wondered. A tidbit of celery? Perhaps a moonbeam that had gotten stuck there during the night. No, neither of those. But whatever it was, what Betsy did next made Fred very uneasy. She dragged the Water Bowl over and began to climb on top of that.

Bad idea! Fred knew from experience that Water Bowls (WBs, which are closely related to WCs) were very tricky items. They seemed innocent enough, sitting there peacefully. But if you just *bumped* a WB, it would go into a panic, leap into the air, and flip upside down.

The way Betsy delicately placed her strong but slender toes on opposite sides of the WB looked promising; obviously she was being careful. Fred also admired how Betsy stood up ever so gracefully, balancing herself with the skill of a circus acrobat.

Up... up... up she stood, and turned slightly, and began to lean into the corner, reaching... reaching higher... h-i-g-h-e-r...

TIP-P-P... p... p...... FLIP... PLOP.... SLOOSH.

Then everything was quiet.

Betsy picked herself out from *under* the Water Bowl and looked down at the puddle of water as it soaked into the shavings. Doesn't history repeat itself, Fred thought, recalling how he'd done the exact same thing a few times himself.

But even before Betsy spoke to him, Fred was standing and offering to help. It was as if he were being guided by invisible strings. Fate. Maybe Bad Luck.

"My dear," he heard himself say, "I might have an Idea how you can reach up much higher."

Betsy turned to him and smiled. Yes, Fred was doing exactly what he was *supposed* to do, she observed. It must be Fate.

So that was how, and why, the Fliffs built a *Living Ladder.*

Fred knelt on the bottom. Sherman—the next biggest Fliff—knelt on his father's back, then Rhoda, then Betsy, then Charlie, and last, and highest, and not the best balanced, was Oyster.

Constructing the Living Ladder was not as easy as it looked. First, because Fred ('Father') was on the bottom and a whole troupe of athletic Fliffs were perched on top of him, he was feeling pretty squashed by the time Charlie climbed up.

Plus, Charlie took his time because he didn't believe in heights. While watching TV with Bert or Chloe, Charlie had seen shows about mountain climbing, sky diving, and circus trapeze acts and absolutely NONE of those activities made any sense to young Charles Fliff. His ancient relatives came from the Jungle, the *floor* of the Jungle, and that was where his roots were. Period. So, needless to say, when it was his turn to climb up, Charlie took his time and climbed carefully. He grabbed a good handful of silky hair, and he really planted a paw so it wouldn't slip as he climbed. And he took his time.

Oyster, on the other hand (or paw), really wanted to zoom up the furry brown wall so she could get way..y..y up there and look around. Her zoomy climb, therefore, was not gentle. Oyster stuck her toe in Sherman's ear, pulled her sister's fur, and kicked Charlie's chin (accidentally). Then, when she did reach the top she looked around much too quickly and got dizzy. Suddenly, with her head spinning and stomach feeling weird, Oyster reached out to grab the cage wall. Bad move. Oyster reached too far, too fast.

That did it. The Living Ladder swayed like a rubber tree in a hurricane. Then it bent, bulged, and popped, squirting Pigs in all directions. Charlie fell on Rhoda, Sherman fell on Mother, and Oyster, shrieking at the top of her lungs, hit someone, bounced, hit someone else, and fell on her father.

The Pigpile had crashed. Fate. Again.

Later, after dinner, Betsy sighed and said, "I wish I could have seen over the top of the cage. Getting around seems like an interesting Idea."

Everyone looked at her strangely. Then Fred winked and said very bravely before he could stop himself, "You will, my dear, you will. Trust me."

CHAPTER 3

IS CHANGE STRANGE?

It was quiet and late in the big old Victorian farmhouse. The Williams adults were asleep, as were their children, Bert and Chloe. The Fliff children were asleep, too, and Mother.

The cage was cool and pleasant. Its walls were made from pine, and the wood smelled good and there were interesting patterns to see in the grain of the wood. Fred liked this time of evening... late in the evening, actually.

So Fred Fliff lay awake and thought about his family's odd experience that day. Everyone (except Charlie) had been so excited by the simplest little Idea. *Getting around*. Although that seemed like a vague Idea, Fred thought it was way more interesting than Square Dancing. Reaching up... *Getting around*... Getting to the top of the cage... wanting to see how things looked from up there.

What puzzled Fred was, all of them had been up and *over* the cage wall when Chloe or Bert took them out to play. Would Betsy's Idea be any different? Fred had a hunch it would be different, and probably nothing easy or simple. Even though Betsy was patient and even-tempered, her manner of thinking was quite complex. Or complicated. Either one.

Fred had a mental picture of how foolish she had looked when the Water Bowl betrayed her. All wet, shavings and pellets stuck to her fine fur, and yet she had not been embarrassed. Not at all. In fact, she had seemed pleased with herself. Why did she want to get to the top? What

19

was up there? And why had the kids been so excited about it?

He had no answers to these questions. All Fred knew was that change had happened. Yes, that was it—*Change*. Life would be different now. The rules would be different. Oh, down would still be *down*, but would up be *Up* in its usual place? What about the Cat, Fred wondered. If Change happened, would the Cat bark, rather than hiss and snarl? Would Thunder the Wolfhound become Tinkle, the Toy Poodle?

Out there in the old Jungle, Change was always changing. Fred understood that fact of life. The innocent-looking vine might actually be a huge SNAKE. The water might look calm, but beneath the surface, are CROCODILES lying around waiting for a careless Guinea Pig to go for a dip? That's how it had always been in the Jungle—Change.

But what about here, Fred wondered. No doubt Change happened here, too, so the question was: Would he be alert to the Change? Would he be able to react smartly and bravely?

He sure hoped so. No doubt this was the new Jungle, and the Fliff family would have to apply their skills. Fred was willing to do that, but again, he hoped he would do a good job. He wanted to be a good father, as his father had been, and he wanted to be a good helpmate to Betsy. The Jungle Fliffs had been explorers (he knew this from *genetic memory*) and mighty defenders of the home. Inventors, too, come to think of it.

Creatures had looked up to the Fliffs of long ago. THERE! Looked *up*. Up to the top! Why not! Okay, so Getting around was going to be good.

As Fred began to slip into sleep, he had another, and very unusual, mental picture. Fred glimpsed someone carrying a light of some kind. They were climbing... down... into a.... Then he fell asleep.

CHAPTER 4

FATHER'S IDEA

The next day was Saturday. Bert and Chloe were outside, skating on the pond at the bottom of Big Hill. Mr. Williams was nearby, cutting firewood. On Saturdays Mrs. Williams went off to visit her mother at The Happy Valley Institute for the Criminally Unhinged.

On a morning like this when the Williams were outside, the Fliffs were free to play Guessing Games or do exercises or sing opera, if they wished (*der Flederpig* was one of their favorites). This morning, however, was different. Why? Because an Idea had taken hold.

After breakfast and clean-up, Fred ('Father') gathered the family to discuss his plan. Betsy ('Mother') sat beside him, the four children facing them. Sherman had a small pad and pencil in case Pop (also called... never mind, you know his first name) asked someone to take notes.

Charlie was hopeless as a note-taker. Too slow, because he thought about every word before writing it, so of course he could never keep up. Oyster was no better. She wrote fast enough, but was a poor speller and she scribbled and no one stood a chance of understanding what she wrote.

Rhoda shut her eyes during Talks like this, so she could make mental pictures of what they were talking about. That was the way Rhoda worked on her Ideas, making pictures in her head. Naturally, she couldn't take notes if her eyes were closed.

So that's why Sherman got stuck with the job of taking notes.

"Mother had an interesting Idea yesterday," Father began. He stood tall, and his deep voice filled the cage with a pleasant rumble. "The Idea about getting to the top of the wall was a new step for us in..."

"You made a joke," Charlie said, interrupting.

Father looked at him, puzzled.

" 'Step' " Charlie explained, "as in 'getting to the *top* of the... ' ".

" '... wall'. I get it, Chaz—'stepping up'. Anyway, I have an Idea of how we can get up the wall without crushing each other. Anyone interested?"

Everyone nodded.

"Okay, here's the Plan: When Chloe and Bert get back, they'll want to play with us on the floor. Good! Under the toy chest and inside the little closet, you'll find painted sticks from that game called, um..."

" 'Build-It' ", Rhoda said.

"That's the one. Whoever goes out, collect one or two pieces like this..." he described the lengths he wanted "...and bring them back into the cage."

"Whoa... o... o," Sherman put in. "Won't Chloe think that's kind of weird, us holding onto those round sticks?"

Father shook his strong head. "Not really. Chloe likes us to play with her toys. In fact, she might help. Collect some couplers, too. They're in a blue box by the corner of the bed."

When asked what the parts were for, Father gave a mysterious reply. "You'll see," he said. "Trust me."

Sherman and Rhoda just looked at each other and rolled their dark brown eyes. Pop's Ideas were a walk on the wild side, sometimes.

But lo and behold, Father had guessed right. After Chloe played with Rhoda and Sherman, and was putting them back in the cage, she saw that Rhoda had held onto two sticks. Being a helpful child, Chloe added to the Fliff's pile of sticks. When she saw that they were also collecting the plastic couplers, she gave them a handful of those, too. In fact, the Fliffs suddenly had too many parts inside the cage, and it was Oyster the Messy One who realized they had a problem.

After dinner (beet stems, lettuce hearts, and multi-grain pellets) the sharp-eyed littlest Fliff pointed to the pile and said, "We got to do something 'bout this pile of stuff," she squeaked. "T'morrow's when Chloe has got to do the things on her floor and stuff, don't forget."

Her brothers and sister all looked at each other and shrugged. They understood what Oyster was getting at, but her mangled descriptions were always a treat.

"What?" Oyster demanded, seeing their expressions. "We should make the... you know, the 'getting up' thing... before it's too late."

Everyone agreed to that. The Fliffs had been called to Action. It was an Idea that got changed to a Plan. But making the 'getting up thing' turned out to be sort of complicated. And *then* what happened was much more complicated than Cats trying to ride Snakes. Seriously.

What happened was, Fred Fliff nearly lost his brave life *in the mountains*! Strange? Yes indeed.

CHAPTER 5

HOW GUINEA PIGS REALLY THINK
(And how all of this adventure started)

· Notions. Ideas. Schemes. Plans... Are these mental activities important to us? Yes, they are. Extremely important. Why? Because these *brain activities*—ideas, plans, and so forth—are the parts and pieces of imagination. And Imagination is how the mind has fun. Imagination is what you can call the Playground of the mind. At least this is how a Guinea Pig's mind works.

(Next week we will talk about how an Ant's mind works. Or maybe a Rhinoceros's.).

Oyster's warning about hiding the collected parts was taken seriously. The Fliffs had to get the cage cleaned up, and fast. As soon as Chloe and Bert went downstairs for dinner, Father quickly showed the family what his Idea was. He put the thing together on the cage floor. "See?" he said. "Change is simple, once you discover the secret." Father was so confident.

But, by golly, Father really did have an Idea. Working at top speed he assembled the sticks and couplers into a... a... ladder? A ladder? Yes, a ladder, and there it was, lying flat as a waffle on the cage floor.

Now what? The Idea was to go Up and Down, not Back and Forth. So what they had to do was lift one end of the ladder and lean it against the cage wall. But not now. Dinner was over and Chloe would be coming back to clean her room **and** the cage. Therefore, the ladder—a real Ladder this time, not a furry Living Ladder—had to be hidden. Where? Oh, that was so easy. The Fliffs hid their Ladder under the shavings and Chloe never noticed anything strange. The Hiding Plan worked! (When you hide something, hide it in plain sight. For example, next time you hide a Camel, hide it with a bunch of other Camels.)

Next day, Sunday, right after lunch, the Williams went outdoors for winter fun—skating, building igloos, making hot chocolate, playing tiddlywinks, and falling down. As soon as their excited voices were far enough away, the Fliffs dug the Ladder out and got ready to go. Up.

The job looked easy enough. Just lift one end of the ladder and lean it against the cage wall. Well, Fred lifted one end and began to walk toward the ladder's other end, to stand the ladder up. That went okay until Fred reached the middle and the *other end* lifted. Now Fred was holding the *entire* ladder over his head and it was horizontal again.

Try again, this time from the opposite end.

Same thing: One end Up, and Up, then BOTH ends UP, like a See-Saw that quits in the middle of the ride.

A very frustrated Father Fliff plopped the misbehaving ladder onto the cage floor and declared that he was going to make a Great Pronouncement. But wait. Charlie ran to the ladder and stood on one end.

"Okay, Pop, try it again. This'll work, trust me." He was grinning from ear to ear (which is spectacular to see when a Pig does it).

Skeptical but willing, Fred began to lift again. Sure enough! He reached the middle and the tricky end had not risen, because there was clever young Charles holding it down. Until... Until Fred walked his end up higher and higher, way past the middle and closer to Charlie, and then it happened. Charlie's end of the ladder suddenly weighed <u>less</u> than the other end and U-P-p-p went Charlie. He went up so fast he couldn't jump off. Up he flew, like an acrobat at the circus. Charlie did not like heights. Then he jumped.

Needless to say, everything came down except Fred's frustration.

Aha, but here's what happens when someone observes the problem and tries another way to fix it. Calm as a cooled cucumber, Betsy went to the ladder, bent over, and pulled the top section off. The children gasped. Oh No, they thought. No more fun watching the Tricky Ladder and the Flying Charlie Trick? No more Up? No more IDEAS?

Hold on, don't give up. Then Mother pulled more of it apart. Soon, the only remaining part of the ladder was a section of four rungs, which she picked up easily. Mother leaned that shortened section against the wall. Easy. Then she got another section and gave it to Fred. "When I climb this short section," she said, "I'll push my section back and you stick your section into the couplers. Then you can climb up and handle the third section, which we'll hand to you, and away you go."

"Away up," he said.

"Precisely, dear."

So that was how the Real Ladder got built, *against* the wall in a vertical posture.

Fred was so excited as he went higher. Climb, push, add a section, climb, push, add another section, climb again. He had a feeling of flying! Higher and higher he went, and the higher he got, the faster he wanted to go....

AND THEN, ALL OF A SUDDEN Fred had reached the very TOP of the CAGE WALL and he was so excited he climbed right up onto the wall... where it was narrow... and he braced himself... and he closed his eyes... and... and... and he **STOOD UP**!

Oh oh. Standing up. That was the exact moment when Fred's world *changed*. In less than a minute he had gone from being a Jungle Pig in a farm house in the winter in Connecticut, a furry pet running around on the floor of a cage, to a Mountain King Pig, standing on a narrow ledge. He opened his dark brown eyes.

O-O-O-O-H-h-h-h-h-h... Mistake.

Fred opened his eyes and he could not see ANYTHING! No walls, no family, no Water Bowl, no safe floor. He was lost. Terrified, he shut his eyes and then peeked. All he could tell was that he was way up high and there was NOTHING to hold onto.

Fred's poor mind went blank. Blank. B-l-a-n-k.

Fred Fliff was **lost** on a mountain top.

This was NOT the kind of change he had hoped for. He knew he had gone up, just as Betsy had wanted. But he'd gone too far. Way too far. Into an Unknown zone where there is nothing. Nothing at all. Just dizziness and being all alone. A wall too far. Oh, what has change done to me, Fred asked. I am lost.

CHAPTER 6

WHY DID I DO THIS!

Fred knew he would have to look again. He just knew it.

But he also knew, from his head to his toes, that he DID NOT WANT TO.

He was more afraid than he had ever been. All he could think of was: *How did this happen to me? HOW?*

A cold wind whispered terrible messages in his ears. "YOU ARE WAY, WAY UP," the wind said. "DO YOU KNOW WHAT HAPPENS WHEN YOU ARE SO VERY HIGH AND ALL ALONE?"

Oh, Fred knew, all right.

He knew *exactly* and in **agonizing** detail what every second of the terribly *l—o—n—g* f—a—l—l would *feel* like.

And what it would *sound* like (**Splat**), and what would happen to his well-rounded, medium brown, slightly ruffled, strong and helpful body when his long plunge came to an

E-

N-

D.

He would **hit bottom**, a *m—i—l—l—i—o—n* miles away, alone, injured, unable to move in the deep snow. And hungry.

THAT IS EXACTLY WHY HE WAS SO SCARED!

So Fred Fliff, frightened, paralyzed with fear, and helpless, used the last of his strength, the very last toe and heel... well, *both* sets of toes and heels... that were barely holding him to the narrow, narrow ridge of mountain... Fred managed to open one eye.

Squeezing his face as tightly as he could, really scrunching it up so he would not see much, Fred let his eye tell him what it saw. **OH NO...**

Oh **YES**! Way far away in the foggy distance were... what? They were things he didn't recognize.

'Maybe... ,' said a small voice inside his head, 'maybe if you looked again, you would... '

'NO! NO! NO!' the *other* little voice shrieked. 'If you look any closer you will F...

A...

L...

L.'

But he couldn't resist. Now that his eye was slightly open, Fred knew he would *have* to look down. When you are going to fall to your doom, the very <u>last</u> thing you want to do is look down. But Fred did look down. The first thing he recognized was a big strong stomach. He couldn't see his toes—they were hiding somewhere beneath that proud but lonely and hungry stomach. Then he looked farther away and everything got blurry. The world disappeared into a blurry, wobbly, fuzzy, weird, confusing, frightening empty space that had no beginning and no end. The Place of No Beginning and No End. At the sound of that dreadful title inside his handsome, keenly chiseled head, Fred's knees wobbled and threatened to collapse. He could feel his body swaying in the wind and he shut his eyes and his head commenced to twirl slowly, like a feather in a dust devil, a hay bale in a tornado, a ship in a whirlpool.

A great Sadness crept into Fred's freezing body. He now understood that *Change* had come and he had NOT been ready for it.

He wished he had done a better job thinking the entire Plan through.

Fred wished he could fly, like a Great Northern Owl or a Red-Tailed Hawk. Even though he would be a Bird, he could fly by a window and talk to his dear family and show them all sorts of aerial tricks. Maybe even give them rides. And Fred the Hawk would protect his family. If Hunter the Cat came by the house, he'd plummet out of the clouds and screech and scare that darned cat. Take THAT, Hunter!

But Fred was a realist. He knew he would not become a mighty Bird warrior and stunt flyer. But perhaps when he did fall, he would land in a soft snowdrift and when he climbed out, his family could come up to the mountains to see him.

Or perhaps they wouldn't.

N... nnnn... n-n-o (teeth chattering from the cold and fear), Fred knew there'd be no m-m-miracles today. He knew deep in his bones how much he would miss his family. They were such fine Pigs, all of them.

Fred Fliff's last thought... as he came to the end... he couldn't hang on any longer... was "HOW did THIS happen?"

Then, from far, far away came a voice. It was a good voice, a distant yet oddly familiar voice. Why would that wonderful little voice be up here in the mountains in the Place of the Ending? Fred forced himself to put on a brave little smile.

Oh, of course. It was Sherman's voice. What was he saying?

'Fall... ' it sounded like.

Well, I'm going to, son.

Louder this time... "FALL, POP. FALL BACKWARDS."

Fred felt a powerful grip on his trembling ankle.

Fred gave in. He had no strength left. He had no other choice.

He *f-*

    e-

       l-

         l-

           l.

CHAPTER 7

FRED WONDERS WHERE HIS JUNGLE IS

"Quite a lot," Fred admitted. His voice was steadier now and he was no longer shivering.

Fred was sitting comfortably on a pile of cedar shavings, with his back against the cage wall. He had just been asked by Betsy if he'd been scared, standing up there on top of the cage wall with nothing to hold onto. "There was so *awful* much space," he continued, "and so little of me. Did I look scared?"

Betsy thought a moment before answering. "Yes, dear," she said, "you did. But it was a **brave** kind of being scared. And don't forget, you actually did take that *first* really big step up."

They were sitting side-by-side in one corner of the cage and the kids were sound asleep in the opposite corner. Chloe was asleep, too, and even the Williams house had settled down for a winter's night rest.

Fred looked over his broad shoulder at Betsy, whose warm and expressive face was softly lit by a small beam of moonlight. He could see enough of her expression to know that she was proud of him, even if he had been scared. He was grateful for the way Betsy always... well, almost always... made him and the children feel important.

"Honestly, dear, I had no choice," he said. "On top of the wall like that, what else could I do except stand up? But that simple action— standing up—produced a very strange effect. Suddenly I was on the very top of a... of a..." Fred had to think about the frightening image "...tall, tall mountain, where it was bitterly cold."

"Oh my," Betsy exclaimed. "Was it like a mountain you had seen in a book?"

"No, not at all. It was so real. And so huge! I could feel the wind and the cold and I couldn't move. There was no place to go... except down." Fred thought again. "You know, dear," he said, nodding as the memory came back, "I wished I could fly. I imagined I was a hawk and for a few moments it felt like I was soaring. Isn't that silly?"

She shook her head—No, not silly.

"Something else, too, Betsy. Even though I was freezing, I kept holding on. I wanted to be with you and the kids..."

Betsy squeezed his paw. Fred squeezed back and continued explaining the extremely odd experience he'd just been through. "I had a dim thought that maybe the *cold world* I was seeing was a new kind of Jungle and I would have to find a way to adjust to it. You see, dear, when you reached up that wall..." he pointed to the spot Betsy had touched when she was on tiptoe "...I sensed that we were going to be changed, that our *lives* would be changed. It was as if that simple act of yours had a profound effect on our lives. Does that make any sense?"

A thoughtful frown crossed her pretty white and tan face as Betsy considered Fred's question. She thought a moment, then answered. "Yes. It makes sense to you, Fred. You see things *differently* from the way I do. You understood that Change has happened. You see a new Jungle, and adventures. I see things we *should* do. You know, like reaching high. I see what our children will become when they are our age." Betsy winked at him. "That's why we were such a good team when we took this first big step."

Fred chuckled. "A team," he said slowly, as if testing the idea. "Well, let me tell you, I was very glad to have our team save me from falling off the edge."

It was Betsy's turn to laugh. "When Sherman grabbed your ankle and yelled for you to fall backward, I knew what was going on in your head. In your moment of extreme danger, it was an act of faith for you to put full trust in Sherman's hands."

Fred nodded and shrugged his powerful shoulders. "I didn't have much choice. He's a very strong lad. Wait a minute... wait. That was the *second* time you said **first** big step. Do you see us taking more steps?"

Mother nodded. "Of course. Didn't I just say that I see what we *should* be doing? We'll take lots more big steps, Mister Fred the Ladder Climber. Well, that was plenty of excitement for this day," she said, yawning. "Good night, dear."

And in a moment, she was sound asleep.

Chloe's room was dark, except for a windowful of moonlight that gently entered the room and painted the top of the cage the softest touch of green and blue and yellow and grey. (Guinea Pig eyes can detect these soft hues, because at night in the Jungle they must be able to recognize such items as leaves, flowers, and snakes.) Fred loved how the colors slid and played amongst themselves. He knew from their studies that colors were made of tiny odd things called *photons* and that the *photons* he was seeing now, right here in the room, might have actually come from the moon! He wondered if the stars he had seen out of Chloe's window sent their light the same way, by photons. If so, goodness, what a long distance they had traveled. Would they be tired, after such a long trip, he wondered. Interesting.

Fred enjoyed the end of the day, when he often stayed awake, listening and thinking. The house had a catalog of squeaks and groans. It was, as Mr. Williams often said when he was fixing something, an *old* house. Fred thought the house was talking softly to its inhabitants, reassuring them that even though its joints were old and stiff, the house was still strong and would protect them.

Fred enjoyed listening to the Outside, too. He knew what most of those sounds were—rain and wind, thunder and lightning, the murmurings of Night Creatures. Creatures, hmmm.

That thought reminded him of Thunder the Dog. Thunder was a Wolfhound, according to what Chloe and Bert said. Wolf. Hound. Pellets alive, that sure sounded scary! The Williams kids didn't seem scared of the Dog, though. In fact, they spoke of Thunder as if he was a friend.

Another Night Creature the Fliffs knew about, and he was NOT a friend, was a Cat named Hunter. Fred had never seen Hunter, but he had heard the Williams family talking about him. What they said about this *Creature of the Night* was not good. No, no, NOT GOOD.

Fred didn't want to think about Hunter, nor about some of the other characters that inhabited the Outside world. What about Big Foot, the Yeti from the mountains of Tibet? Want to meet him? Not yet, thanks. Those 33-foot long Anacondas that lived in swamps? Godzilla? Father had seen all of them on TV and he had no desire to see them up close and personal.

In fact, the Outside was mostly a mystery to the Fliffs. They had seen things on TV and in books, but they knew that real life out there was different. All in all, Outside seemed like a frightening place, but fascinating, too. Fred wanted to see what it really looked like. He wondered, though, if he might be too cautious to explore the Outside. Would they have to deal with all those strange characters, like Snakes? Or the terrible plant that had a girl's name? Something like Aubrey. Audrey? Oh well, no need to worry about that.

As he was drifting off to sleep, Fred experienced something very odd. It was a feeling of floating and drifting, of gliding and walking in soft grass. Yes, that was it—he was in the Outside. He could smell grass, hear sounds, and in this peculiar vision of dream-traveling, he knew exactly where he was going.

... it was dark, but not pitch black... and he was standing on grass and there was a ladder sticking out of a hole in the ground. Oh Pigsters, that was weird! But even weirder, the hole in the ground had been carefully made and light was coming out of it. An orange-ish light that flickered and wavered and it seemed... it seemed **friendly!** It did. Father wanted to climb down the hole in the ground.

Then the vision floated away and before you could say 'Toasted Pellets,' the darkness surrounded him and Fred drifted into the comfortable embrace of family and being safe.

Just before he slipped away to sleep, Fred smiled. He had survived the first big Change. Not bad for a Pig who nearly fell off a mountain.

CHAPTER 8

A BALLOON TRAPEZE? (How odd.)

Monday mornings were usually quiet in the house, because the People were away. In fact, as Betsy thought about getting up and starting chores, she felt the tiniest bit bored. The Great Wall Adventure had been exciting and what she *really* wanted to do was climb to the top of the cage and walk all the way around the edge, then jump off into a big pile of soft shavings.

But... Y-yawn... that was kind of a nutty Idea and anyway, the ladder was safely hidden under the shavings.

Those were Betsy's thoughts as she opened her glimmering dark eyes and saw two strange... no, two *ultra* strange things. First, all four children were watching her and grinning like fools. And two, there was the ladder, propped up against the wall. And next to it, near the top, was a small platform.

Wait... *three* ultra-strange things! Fred was **nowhere** to be seen. Gone. Disappeared. Absent. Away. Not here! Her mouth fell open. Betsy tried to speak, but couldn't.

Understanding her mother's problem, Rhoda said, quite calmly, "Um, Mom, I have some news. Pop has gone over the edge."

"Well," Mother sputtered, "he certainly has! And... and..."

Oyster began to giggle. "It's a sup... rise. Pop said to tell you."

"What on Earth is going on?" Mother demanded, in a voice colored with dismay.

"Not going *on,*" Rhoda replied gleefully. "Going *down!* Come on up the ladder. Let's see for ourselves."

"See? See what, for goodness sake?" Mother exclaimed, astonished and bewildered. "Rhoda, I would appreciate the courtesy of being informed about this... this... whatever it is. And I really want to know where your father is!"

Seeing that her mother was worried about Pop, and a little angry, too, Rhoda looked over at Sherman for help. He shrugged helplessly.

Same with Charlie, only more helplessly.

Oyster? The youngest Fliff was bouncing and pointing. She wanted to go up the ladder and see for herself. But she wouldn't spill the beans. (Everything else, but not the beans.)

Mother got the picture. She would have to go along with this silliness if she wanted to find out what *really* was happening. "Alright," she said wearily. "But I expect someone to catch me if I fall off that... that device."

If it was Surprise Time inside the cage, it was the same *outside* the cage. Fred Fliff, the Great Surpriser, was dangling from a climbing rope and wondering if he could hold on any longer. It was a long way to the floor. A long, LONG way, and his arms were getting very tired.

In fact, all of Fred felt tired. He tried to look directly below, to see where he would land if he fell. No luck. All he could see was the now-familiar round, muscular stomach. Then he tried to look *up* his climbing rope and he couldn't do that, either. His head was sort of jammed between the rope and the cage wall. Oh oh, what now? he asked himself.

Keep going, he told himself. Though his body seemed heavier, and his grip on the rope less strong, Fred lowered himself carefully, paw over paw, until an outstretched toe touched something... THE FLOOR!

"The Pig has landed," he whispered victoriously, wishing he could think of something more stirring to say. No matter, he was **On The Floor. By himself!** Fred scanned the territory. Oh Wow, how different the room looked, without Chloe or Bert here. This is the Bedroom Jungle, he said to himself. There's no protection now, old fellow. You're on your own.

The room was **huge**. That was the bed. Okay, and that's the bedspread hanging off the side. It looked like a giant sail that had fallen down, or a cloth icicle. Was anything behind it? He could see dim and vague shapes in the darkness under the bed. He'd never seen *them* before. Did that one move? Were those green things eyes? Did he hear something growl? (He did. It was his stomach.)

Remembering the Survival Rules of Jungle Life, Fred carefully studied the surroundings. Ah, there was the toy box. Under that was a large space where a clever Pig could hide. And over there, Chloe's bureau—same thing; maybe even room for a Workshop.

Fred scooted behind the table leg. Peering around it, he saw the door to the closet. It was partially open. Through the small gap, Fred could see inky blackness. He knew that Bert was a little bit scared of the closet, because he said it lead to a Secret Cave where Dragons lived.

Dragons ? Dragons probably weren't real.

From what Fred knew about Dragons, he doubted that the Williams house was big enough to hold a full-sized one, the kind with wings and fire in its mouth. Still, it might be a good idea to avoid the closet until... well, you know... until later.

Fred was just glancing over at the bedroom door, which was fully closed, when he heard a distant voice floating down from the sky... er, from up above. Golly, was that far away!

When Betsy was level with the top of the wall the first thing she saw: a hook that had been jammed into the wood. A rope was attached to it. Then she knew what Fred had done. He had made a special climbing hook which was attached to a climbing rope. Clever. Unless the hook slipped. Or the rope broke. Then not so clever.

Betsy climbed the rest of the way up and peeked over the edge, at the floor. Yup, there was the rope, but no Fred.

"Freddie," she called in a strong whisper, "where are you?"

What to her wondering eye should appear, way down there, but a small, recognizable figure who stepped out onto the rug, turned, and looked up.

"**Hi ho,**" the jaunty explorer called up. "**You're so-o-o far away!**" Fred cupped his paws around his mouth. "**Can you hear me**?" he called.

"Of course I can hear you, Fred. What is this thing called?"

"**A grappling hook. Useful, isn't it?**"

"Very. Are you going to grapple your way back up here?"

Fred laughed jauntily. He'd been waiting for this. "I'm glad you asked," he shouted. "It's my way home."

Seeing Betsy up there did give Fred a twinge of doubt. If his arms had gotten tired going *down* the rope, how would they cope with going *up*? But Pigs always move ahead, he reminded himself.

Up top, Betsy was shaking her head in disbelief. All this Getting Up and Down business was making her nervous. Rhoda did nothing to cure her nerves when she said, "Keep watching, Mom, you ain't seen nothin' yet!"

Rhoda was on the platform.

"Oh good," Mother sighed. "Slang from watching TV and now I have something new to worry about." She looked around Rhoda. "Gracious, how nice to see the rest of you up here."

Surprise! Now, five curious Pigs watched as Father began the next grand adventure.

Fred started by tying the end of the Climbing rope, or line, to his belt. Then he headed directly to Chloe's bed. He looked up. Overhead were six strings and above them, six very large, bright yellow, helium-filled balloons. They'd been there for two days. Chloe had gone to a birthday party and her prize for winning some game was the six balloons. There they were, still tightly pressed against the ceiling.

The onlookers wondered if... or what... or why.

Fred knew. Not able to reach a string by standing on tiptoes, he pulled a toy fire engine over and hopped up on the cab. He stood carefully and tried again. This time he got a string. And then two more. Holding on to the strings, he jumped off the fire engine cab and sank gently to the floor.

Back on the cab and grab the last three strings. Fred now had all six balloons under his control. Everyone watched with amazement as he expertly tied a small dowel to the strings and then, holding onto the stick like an acrobat on a giant trapeze, Father leapt off the fire truck and FLOATED above the floor.

The kids cheered. Mother clapped.

In short order, Father became an expert at swinging on his balloon trapeze, and by swinging in one direction he could make the balloons follow along. Now came the tricky part. By pulling down hard and running and jumping, Fred was able to bounce and swing at the end of the strings. After three tries, he was so good at this that he took an extra long run and bounced himself right up onto Chloe's bed. It was a FABULOUS stunt, and he had another trick up his sleeve!

"Here's the deal," he yelled over. "When I jump off the bed, start pulling me. If I'm lucky, I'll make it all the way to the cage. Here I come... PULL, PULL, PULL!"

Quick as bunnies, the Fliffs grabbed the grappling hook off the cage wall and climbed down to the cage floor and began pulling. All of a sudden they heard a THUMP up top. They all looked up and there was a paw, and a second paw, then the tippity top of a wonderful tan and white and brown head, and also up there, bumping against the ceiling were six very large bright yellow balloons. Father was home again! Almost.

"Keep pulling," a familiar voice called. "I need a lift."

They did, and five strenuous minutes later a grateful Fred was standing on wobbly but happy legs, with his family, on the cage floor.

"**We did it!**" he shouted, hugging all of them. "We got out of the cage and navigated the entire bedroom *by ourselves*! It was your idea, dear," he said to Betsy. "Hmmm, and speaking of ideas, all that climbing and ballooning gave me an appetite. I could use a snack and a nice nap."

Sherman looked at his father and grinned broadly. "You can have my beet stem, Pop," he said. "And, uh, would it be okay if I took a ride?"

"Ride?" At first Father didn't understand. But when he saw children grinning and pointing up, he got it.

So began a frolicking hour of Balloon Trapezing. Sherman tried it first. He climbed part way down the line and grabbed the dowel that was tied to the six balloon strings. Quick as a wink he was swinging wildly around the room. Then the other kids clamored for a turn. Soon the children were trying to outdo each other, by running faster and jumping farther and one by one, each succeeded in stretching the Leap and Bounce Rides around Chloe's room.

Mother and Father were careful, though, to be sure that the Safety Line was always connected, so the Trapeze artist could be hauled back when the ride had ended.

Mother took to Ballooning, since she was graceful and quick. Cautious Charles managed the cleverest trick of all. By careful timing, he was able to swing out from the cage wall and come back, without being tugged by the Safety Line.

By now all the Fliffs were energized. On Oyster's next turn, she was determined to try the Biggest Stunt of All. Sherman knelt on the top of the wall. Oyster got way back and ran as fast as she could. She jumped up onto her brother's strong back, and out, out into space. Oh, how Oyster flew!

Oh, but there was a catch. Charlie had been studying how Oyster had made her great leap forward and he failed to notice that her climbing line was loosely draped atop of the cage wall. Right where Charlie stepped. Oyster leapt into the air and her line followed. And it kept following until it came to the loop around Charlie's ankle. Then Charlie took off like a rocket, foot first. What a daring circus act!

Luckily, Charlie's wild flight ended with him crashing, unharmed, into Samantha Valkyrie, Chloe's favorite doll. The doll suffered no damage, either.

But then, as Oyster's ride continued, once Charlie was off her line, there came two loud noises.

BAM...... BAM

Oyster felt the Trapeze shudder and drop, but she held tightly and flexed her small knees, ready to absorb the impact in case she hit the floor. (All Guinea Pigs are born with Survival Reflexes like that.) The Trapeze sank more and more, and Oyster was still swinging at a fast speed. If she hit the floor, flexed knees or not, the small child would be injured.

Oh oh! But at the last possible second, the remaining four balloons began to lift the child. Oyster stretched her strong little legs out in front of her and z-z-z-oooomed safely to the top of the arc, and back, and forward again, and finally she came to a stop, dangling one inch above the floor.

It took quite an effort to tug the brave little Creature home. And just as she was safely over the top of the cage wall, a third yellow balloon burst. **BAM**.

Trapeze Ballooning was over.

Which is exactly what Father said.

But Sherman corrected him. "Not quite, Pop," he said, pointing at the ceiling.

They all looked up, just as Father started to say "Wha..."

He didn't have to finish the question. The answer was right there, for everyone to see. EVERYONE, including Chloe, Bert, Mr. and Mrs. Williams, and the entire neighborhood. Three perky yellow balloons were up against the ceiling, while three collapsed balloons dangled from the trapeze bar like wet socks. Everyone's mouth flopped open. They all understood immediately—they had a problem.

Suddenly Father snapped his fingers. "Got it!" he exclaimed.

(Well, what he *got* was—up to now—the most complicated and daring Idea the Fliffs had ever come up with. If you promise not to tell any of the little kids, here is what he did. First, the Fliffs made three arrows out of thin sticks. Then they made a bow. Then they pulled the surviving balloons close to the cage and shot arrows at them. Bam, Bam, Bam. Then they untied the trapeze bar and tossed the Limpies over the cage wall. Then Father raced down the Climbing Line, grabbed the six Limpies, and hid them way in back, under Chloe's toy box. Then he ran back to the Climbing Line and just had enough strength to get back up to the cage.)

"We won't say another thing about them," he cautioned his family. "If anyone ever asks us, we'll just say the Cat did it."

That was the end of Balloon Flying.

(Chloe blamed Bert and Bert, making a joke, said the Pigs did it.

Yeah, sure, Bert. Ha ha.

CHAPTER 9

GOING UP? (Charlie has an Idea.)

When the crisis was all over—when all traces of trapeze and balloon pieces and crazy rides were over, and when the ladder and climbing line were safely hidden—only then did the Fliffs breathe a sigh of relief. Father had NOT fallen off his imagined mountain. They HAD learned how to get out of the cage. And they had become TRAPEZE artists. All in all, quite an accomplishment. However, they were worried about the deflated balloon corpses and Fred and Betsy had an inkling that the Outside World was not always going to be soda and pretzels.

When they heard doors slam downstairs they knew Chloe was home. Fred winced (which is interesting to see) and kicked some more shavings over the hidden gadgets. Seconds later Chloe came flying up the front stairs. She burst into her room and ran over to the cage. The Fliffs took a deep breath and tried to make believe they were thinking about something, like food or maybe an algebra problem.

Chloe peeked into the cage. "HI PIGGIES," she yelled, and ran off.

The Fliffs looked at each other and dared to breathe again. Not a word from Chloe about the missing balloons. Now they'd have to wait for the *rest* of the family. But at least they were over the first hurdle.

After dinner, Bert came in to say Hi to the Fliffs, then he left. Not a word about the balloons. Finally the Fliffs relaxed and had their dinner (pellets and carrots). It was a quiet dinner. When they were through and had cleaned up, done their teeth, and everything in the house was quiet, Father asked, in a very low, soft voice, "Why is everyone so quiet?"

No one had anything to say, which was unusual. Finally, Mother nodded and tilted her sleekly arched brow. "I think I understand, dear," she said slowly. "You see, we had such fun and suddenly it's all over. Now we have to face the cold, hard fact that we won't be ballooning anymore. It is too dangerous. I think all of us are feeling a let-down..."

"Let. Down," Father interrupted. "A joke."

Mother laughed. "I said it that way on purpose. Anyway, I had such fun on that silly trapeze." Mother made a funny gesture of holding on and swinging through the air. "But we don't **dare** let our People family know about these adventures. We can not get caught! That's all I have to say, Fred. G'night everyone," she whispered.

So saying, Mother curled up and was asleep in seconds. The kids did the same.

Well, that certainly was fast, Father said to himself. From a grand adventure, to feeling let down, to an audience of snoozers. Wow, what a fun crowd, he lamented.

Father decided to stay up a little longer so he could think about the day. Picturing how they had all looked, trapezing wildly around the room, feet stretched out in front of them, jumping, leaping into space... LEAPING OFF THE CAGE WALL, for gosh sake. Father had to laugh. It sure had been exciting. But Betsy was right about not getting caught in some wild escapade. That would be *awful*. It would mean going to Chloe's school for Show & Tell. It would mean TV interviews. But mostly it would mean no more freedom to explore on their own. That would be very sad.

As he pictured himself explaining things in front of the TV camera, he began to get sleepy. Then Father dozed off, half-remembering a distant dream about a strange hole in the ground.

The next day went quietly. The Fliffs did their lessons and chatted and snacked, but throughout the day, one Fliff or the other would glance up at the ceiling or the top of the cage wall and sigh.

Very late that next night, when the train whistle and the big Owl were talking to each other, the Fliffs should have been sound asleep.

But they weren't. They were fidgeting. Finally, in the dark at the bottom of the cage, one of them just had to say something.

"You ain't giving up, are you?" a small voice asked. It was Charlie.

" 'aren't'," Oyster piped up, correcting her younger brother.

"You have an idea?" Sherman asked quietly.

Mother of course heard all this and she wondered why Chaz had asked the question. Yes, Charlie would have Ideas, but not about trapezes or balloons or ladders, because the youngster did not like heights. Imagine her surprise, then, when her younger son announced...

"Yes I do," Charlie whispered to Sherman. "I got a **Plan**. You know, for getting around."

Sherman was skeptical. "A what?" he asked.

"A Plan," Charlie repeated, in a more confident voice. "I do. No kidding."

The fact was, young Charles actually liked the idea of *Getting Around.* It was the flying part, and walking on top of the cage wall, he did not care for. And he was particularly disinterested in going up in the air at the end of silly—**and fragile**--balloons.

"Oh," everyone said, "GREAT! What is it?"

"We should make an elevator," Charlie declared. "It would be faster and W-A-Y safer. Trust me, I know how to do it."

Five happy votes brightened the darkness at the bottom of the cage. (Five Yeses.)

BINGO, just like that, a plan was hatched.

The next morning, instead of lessons, the Fliffs collected pencils, paper, and their notes from Physics class. They had to check a few figures about Mechanical Advantage, pulleys, ratios, and that lecture about 'Tensile Strength of Ordinary Strings and Wires'. Nothing fancy, such as Quantum Uncertainty. (Which no one was certain about, anyway.)

By the end of the week, the elevator plans were complete. All the Fliffs had to do now was find materials, and for this they began work to launch a **MACE**, a **Ma**jor **C**ollecting **E**xpedition.

Saturday arrived at last. The house was empty of Williams, who were off to see Mrs. Williams' father, who was spending two years at a nearby federal institution. No sooner had the front door closed, the Fliffs were ready to go. But before leaving the cage, Mother and Father, together, delivered a clear message to the children:

"Pay attention outside the cage. If you see, hear, smell, or sense danger, give the Alarm Whistle twice, then hide. Otherwise, proceed calmly. Don't run around like wild Salmon. Each of you knows where to find the necessary pieces. Collect quickly and head home. Agreed?"

51

Oh absolutely! the children replied in gleeful unison. You bet! Count on us! Calmly! Hide! Don't worry! Ten-four!

It was an amazing sight, those six brave GPs going up the ladder, over the edge, and down the lines. Six Pigs, including Charlie! No way was he going to listen to Oyster bragging about her *Ex-pet-it*... thing.

Once his slim feet touched solid ground, he instantly forgot his mild fear of heights and made a dash to the bed, where he knew hunting for parts would be good.

However, Mother, Sherman, Rhoda, and Oyster experienced the same initial shock that Pop had, when he was all alone on the floor the first time. The ceiling was higher, the bed larger, and even Chloe's desk looked somewhat like a windowless fortress when seen from below. But they were together, which helped.

Oyster was shivering a little, so Mother asked if she felt all right.

"I guess," the youngest said in a wavering voice. "I wouldn't wanna be, uh, stranded down here."

"Not to worry," Father boomed. "Piece of cake. Quite uneventful down here, once you're used to it. You'll see. Ready, Team?"

Ready? Ha! Does a Pigeon eat seeds? Team ready! Quick as a flash, Father and Sherman were heading for the closet, where they knew several old construction sets had been stored. Rhoda had another destination. "See you soon," Father said to the others, over his shoulder, as they reached the closet door.

Mother watched them march confidently right up to the door, heave it open, and in went Father and Sherman, not hesitating a moment.

Rhoda headed for the toy chest. Charlie had already gone beneath the bed.

"I'm going to the back of Chloe's desk, dear," Mother said to Oyster. "Do you want to come with me?"

Oyster looked around the huge, strange room. "Not yet, Mom," she said. "My toe is sore. Soon's it's better, I'll go with Charlie."

Mother understood. "Certainly," she said. "I'll be working close to Rhodie. If you have a question, just whistle. You know how to whistle, don't you?" That was a little joke. All GPs know how to whistle.

So there the smallest Fliff was, all by herself. Looking around again. Maybe Chloe's room didn't seem quite as large now. Oyster knew eggzakly where everyone was. She could signal for help... and she could hear Charlie, busy at work under the bed, finding all kinds of stuff. She listened. Now it's quiet under the bed... no, she heard Charlie giggle. Not fair! He was gonna get everything on *his* list and make fun of her because she'd be empty-handed. The big Wonkily show-off!

The more Oyster thought about it, the madder she got. She could picture them at dinner and everyone would be bragging *Oh what a great job you did, Charlie, con-grad-you-late-shuns.* Then he'd wait 'til no one was looking and he'd stick his tongue out at her. Well, to heck with you, Mister Smarty Pants Charles. Here I come! Cautiously she walked toward the bed, watchful for ghosts or alligators. Nothing leapt out at her. Oyster got to the bed leg. So far, so good.

"Gee, this is fun," Oyster whispered to herself. She took a step under the bed. "I'm gonna get a prize for finding my stuff," she whispered.

Oyster bent down to look farther under the bed. It was awfully quiet. She wondered where that rotten Charlie was.

"Oh, wonnerful," Oyster said to herself, "there's a piece... wait, I see... something..."

Oyster went farther in and was reaching for something, when... "EEEE—YOW!" The child's shriek was loud enough to be heard at the South Pole. She leapt backwards, did a backwards double-flip, turned to run, tripped over the fire engine. The siren went off... **AaaaA—rRrrr—ahhhh-AaaaaraA.** She made the mistake of looking back under the bed. *HORRORS!*

It was awful. It was a huge horrible monster and it was REAL. It had red eyes like FIRE, and gigantic TEETH and it made an awful gnashing, growling sound and it WAS COMING FOR HER. Its red eyes pinned the helpless child to the floor, like a bug on a pin. Oyster was doomed. She could almost feel the Monster jumping up and down on her 'abba-men.'

No... wait. A Fliff never gives up. Never! Pop said that lesson comes from the Book of Guinea Pig Rules of... well, of *something*. Oyster sprang to her four fleet feet and made a desperate dash for safety. Of course it wasn't such a great idea to run with her eyes closed, but she couldn't look at the thing again.

WHAM. She ran into Pop, who was running to help her. Oyster didn't stop. She sprinted across the room to the nearest Climbing Rope and up she went, like a Pig on a rocket. Over the edge she flew, and down the ladder, right into a pile of shavings. Then she held her breath so she could

hear if the Monster was coming after her. Only then, safe at home and listening with both ears, did Oyster realize that something was very, very wrong. She wasn't hearing shouts or the Fliff family fighting a terrible Monster... no, not at all.

Oyster was hearing **laughter,** and plenty of it. She got out of the shavings and went to the ladder and began to climb, ever so slowly. At the top of the wall she poked her head over and looked down. What she saw completely astonished her. Completely.

Everyone... Mom, Pop, Sherm the Worm, and Rhoda were rolling around on Chloe's floor, laughing like Loons. Oyster realized that her family had gone off the deep end. That was awful. With them lost in LaLa Land, she was going to be very lonely. Oyster wondered if she would have to take care of her family from now on. It would be hard work, but she and Rhodie could boss Sherm and Chaz around. That'd be cool.

First, however, she would have to get rid of the Monster. Oyster thought about it. Maybe she could open the front door of the house and call Hunter the Cat. Let *him* take care of the Monster.

But wait. Then who'll get rid of the durn Cat?

Life had gotten very complicated.

CHAPTER 10

THE SMALL ARE BRAVE, TOO

They were still laughing! WERE THEY ALL CUCKOO NUTTY FRUITCAKES? Oyster could not believe her eyes!

Her FAMILY—four of them—were rolling on the floor, laughing their foolish heads off, AND THE HORR'BLE MONSTER WAS COMING OUT. IT WAS UN'NER THE BED AN' IT WAS GONNA GET 'EM.

Well, no way was Oyster going to let some Terrible Robot Creature attack *her* family. No! Way! She hurled herself over the top of the cage and began to slide down the line to the floor.

Meanwhile, on the floor and rolling around egg'zakly as Oyster had seen them, was her family, and no wonder they were laughing. Father had come dashing into Chloe's bedroom— expecting the worst, having heard Oyster's scream of terror—just in time to have the smallest Fliff crash right into him, knock him over, and keep on going. Father watched in amazement as his daughter set a new world record for Climbing Up the Rope.

And then there were Mother, Rhoda, and Sherman, standing there with their mouths open, not knowing what was going on.

And then, as four Fliffs looked at each other in TOTAL puzzlement, out from under the bed comes Charlie, laughing so hard he couldn't talk. Then they all turned and looked up to the cage and there, at the top of the wall, were eight delicate paw tips, a small head whose hair was standing straight up, like a mop that had been

57

kissed by lightning, and two big black eyes peering fearfully down at them.

That was it. Too much. Everyone burst into wild laughter.

Then Charlie, still laughing, ran back under the bed. **"Watch this,"** he shouted over his shoulder.

In a second everyone could hear a clanking, grinding, whirring, buzzing, hissing noise. Then they saw bolts of crazy blue light and

dangerous red eyes flashing on and off. And then they saw the THING itself, a MONSTER, a ROBOT, a WICKEDLY UGLY MECHANICAL CREATURE coming toward them. It was flexing its mighty metal arms, clacking its sharp claws, and biting with its iron teeth. This was ONE NASTY DUDE and it was coming after the Fliffs!

That was egg'zackly the moment when Oyster had overcome her fear and plunged down the climbing rope to rescue her family. Without thinking of her own safety, the brave little Pig let the rope run through her strong little paws as she dropped, almost out of control, to the floor. Sure, the rope hurt her paws, but SO WHAT!

The child hit the floor, gathered her muscles into powerful little Attack Springs, and sped across the floor at the MONSTER. Growling and shouting the Fliff Victory Cry, **"FLIFF FURRY FURY!"** Oyster was going to torpedo the MONSTER with her round, speeding, brown and beige body.

But then, to her total and complete astonishment, the MONSTER stopped in its tracks and said, in a distorted but familiar voice, *"Hi, Oyster. Havin' fun?"*

Oyster skidded to a stop. She looked at the horrible robot. Something... some one... was in back of the MONSTER. Oyster moved to the side to get a better look....

WHAT?

IT WAS CHARLIE! He was kneeling on the floor with a box in his hands and some kinda cable going from the black box to the back of the MONSTER.

Then, suddenly, Oyster understood everything. She was not a complete fool. *Now* she knew why the Monster had stopped. Now she knew what the box was and what her brother was doing. Now she knew why he was laughing. And why everyone else was laughing. They were laughing at her! They were laughing at her because she had been scared silly by a toy! A toy robot that Charlie had found under the bed!

Then, in that moment of awful discovery which all children experience sooner or later, Charlie understood something, too. He wasn't hearing any more laughter. When the laughing stops like that and suddenly it is very, very quiet, you know, you just KNOW, that you are in BIG D-E-E-E-P TROUBLE. Charlie dropped the Robot Control Box. Everyone looked at him. He knew he was wrong and he didn't know what to do.

Now, some kids... you know one or two kids like this... some kids who *know* they're in trouble, they think fast and blame someone else for doing it! *'He made me do it,'* they yell, and then they start crying and pointing the finger. *'He did! It wasn't my fault.'*

Charlie was tempted to make an excuse. He almost said, 'Gee, you didn't hafta get so scared, Oyster, you knew it was a joke.' Blaming her, in other words. But Charlie didn't do that. No, he didn't. "I guess I scared you," he said slowly, ashamed. "And you were really brave, coming after the Robot like that." Charlie gulped, took a deep breath and said, "I'm sorry, Oyster, no kidding."

Oyster, up to that very second, had been ultra-angry. She was mad at her brother and she knew how silly she must have looked, yelling like that and running away. But when she saw the expression on Charlie's face, some of her anger melted. Some, not all.

"That was a mean trick, Charlie," she said. "I banged my knee when I was running. I knocked Pop down. And that nasty old rope hurt a lot. *Darn* **you!**"

Charlie wiped his nose. What a bad idea it had been, scaring a little kid like that. "If your paws are sore," he said, as a small tear trickled down his brown little cheek, "I can do chores for you tomorrow."

Oyster had to giggle. Charlie looked like a Puppy Dog that has chewed up Uncle Ned's slippers. "That's okay," she said to him. "At least you didn't make up any 'squ'ses.'"

Charlie looked up just as Mother hugged his sister. Then, to Charlie's astonishment, Pop came over and put his arm around the boy's shoulder and said, "You did the right thing just now," Father said. "Apologizing. I'm proud of you. Now, let's go build an elevator."

Which is exactly what they did.

The Fliffs actually built and tested a real ELEVATOR. They did. They worked in the Secret Workshop and made the neat little machine. Everyone tried it out. They were able to go up to the cage from the floor by turning the elevator handle. Get to the floor by the line, get back up in the Elevator. They practiced for an hour and then hid the Elevator under the table. Then back in the cage for some kibbles.

Then something strange happened. Instead of being excited and proud of their work, they were kind of quiet. It was mealtime but no one had any appetite (which was VERY unusual). No one made any jokes. There were lots of sighs and yawns. Finally, Sherman couldn't take the mopey, glum, subdued, quiet, dejected stuff anymore. "WHAT'S WRONG WITH THIS FAMILY?" he demanded, looking around the cage.

Rhoda stood, walked over, and looked him in the eye. "I'll tell you what's wrong, big brother," she said. "What's wrong is, all the great work we did, like the Balloon rides, and the Robot Monster, and building the Elevator, so what? We can go up and down from the cage to the floor and the floor to the cage. So. What!"

Well, that made Sherman mad. He was the one who had designed the Elevator. "Oh yeah," he jeered. "Oh yeah? Well, I s'pose you got a better idea, Rhodie."

Rhoda made a face. "I do. I just don't think you're ready for it, big brave Sherman."

Well, Sherman was really mad by now. Not mad at his sister. He was *frustration* mad. (This happens a lot with Guinea Pigs. They want to go to the Mall or something, but they don't know how to get out of the cage. That is frustrating and it makes them **mad**!)

"Oh yeah?" Sherman said harshly to his sister. "Try me! Make my day! Go ahead, see if your Idea is any good. I dare you!"

Rhoda broke into a knowing smile. She was ready for that dare.

61

CHAPTER 11

RHODA'S IDEA

Eight minutes after the town Bell Tower rang midnight, the Get-It Team of Frederick and Sherman Fliff went over the edge of the cage and down, down into the dark. They were on a scavenging mission. The two treasure hunters wore rubber-soled boots (salvaged from some of Bert's action-hero figures) so their feet would make no sound on the oak floors. They wore black clothes so they could blend with the shadows. They carried tiny flashlights, pencils and pieces of paper, and emergency food. And they spoke in what is called "Pig Whisper", a special squeak-code so soft that a Two-Leg can not hear it. They knew where they were going and what they were after. *"Into the dark, brave went stealthily these fearless gatherers."* (That is a line from the old and famous book of poetry about Guinea Pigs, *We Seek, We Usually Find*, by Phylamunder L. Topperstay.)

Double-checking to be certain that Chloe was sound asleep, the Team slipped through the door and out into the hallway, where they paused, listened, and looked. These Seek and Find Pigs were stealthy and careful, as all Guinea Pigs are in the Jungle. Their first destination: the Sewing Room.

The Sewing Room was in the rear of the house, beside the Attic stairs and the *dark passageway to the cellar*. This was not a popular part of the house, because of moaning noises that could be heard in the attic, and clanking sounds rumbling up the back stairs. Many times the

Fliffs had heard Mr. Williams tell Chloe or Bert that the noises were only an "old house complaining about aches and pains. Wind causes the moans and ancient hurricane chains cause the clanks. Don't worry. Trust me."

Oh sure, Dad, murmured Bert and Chloe, who totally skeptical. They knew what the noises *really* were. (Take a guess. G_ _ _ _ s.)

The Fliffs, however, knew that Mr. Williams was right. They had learned what the house sounds were and they knew the difference between Creature noises and the sounds of lifeless things that moved in the night, like wind and chains.

How could the Fliffs tell the difference? Because Life in the Jungle had taught *all* Guinea Pigs how to understand noise *patterns*. For example, the moans caused by wind are steady patterns, rising and falling everywhere at the same time and in the same way. On the other hand, wet moany noises from a hungry giant Anaconda would be l—o—n—g, low, and very slow. A Tyrannosaurus rex would make loud, grunty, huffing noises, and dripping saliva would make a splashy noise. The Fliffs knew these things and knew there were no ghosts. Goats, yes, but no ghosts.

Oh, sure, there were strange night noises in the Williams house. Mice, for example. And the giant wolfhound, Thunder, had come inside once, downstairs. (Speaking of strange noises—you could hear Thunder's bark a mile away, he was so big and powerful.) One night during the summer, Father Fliff had heard a feline prowling the hall. Not good, especially if it was Hunter. All the Outdoor birds knew Hunter, and they sounded the alarm whenever he was around.

The Fliffs knew that Cats are the most care-ful when they are hunting. They pull their claws back when they walk on hard surfaces. But what Cats can **not** hide is the swishing of their tails. When a Cat is hunting, its tail makes an impatient whispery noise--Swish, Swish. All Pigs know this. On this night, listening carefully, the Team detected no strange *patterns* of noises.

To move safely in the dark, Father showed Sherman how to move in the dark according to the Rules of the Jungle: Go—Stop—Listen. It was easy to learn, Sherman found. He took a step when his father did, stopped at the same time, and listened. It made the lad proud that he could follow Pop's instructions so precisely. They got to the Sewing Room, confident that there were no nasty Creatures in the vicinity.

"It's nice and warm in here," Sherman said, when they were safely inside the little room. "But it certainly is a strange room, isn't it, Pop?"

"Strange is right. Over there..." Father shone his tiny light on a crooked wall "...is the chimney. That keeps the room warm. Over here is where I think the cloth is stored. You know what to look for?"

Sherman gave a low Pig whistle, which meant Yes.

"Good," Father said. "See what you can find. I'm going after thread, needles, and something sharp. If you need help, whistle. You know..."

"I know, Pop," Sherman said. "The Alarm Code."

Father trusted his son to be careful, so off he went to the sewing table for what they would need, while Sherman made his way to the scrap pile in the closet.

The hunting was easy this night. A quick climb and prying open of three drawers gave Fred what he needed. Needles, nylon thread, and a fabric slicer went into his backpack. Sherman was able to pull large scraps of fabric from a bin until he had enough for the project. In just minutes they were back at the door, ready to return to Chloe's room. Father checked outside for noises—none—and turned to his son.

"We're in no rush. Let's have some carrot tea and a small snack."

Sherman needed no second invitation. He closed the door again, while his father folded some cloth for two seats. Then he got the goodies out of his knapsack. In seconds, anyone with good ears might hear a soft crunching noise— crisp pellets being chewed—and a polite sip of carrot tea. All the Fliffs had good manners and chewed with their mouths closed. Nice.

The two Fliffs, sitting comfortably in the warm sewing room, enjoyed the snack and sip. Father liked working with his son. Sherm was a quiet lad, confident but plenty careful, too. And smart. Sherman could figure things out. He took his time at a task and when he came up with an answer, Father knew that it would be right.

As for Sherman being with his father, why it just plain made him swell up with pride when he could help his father. Especially with some of Pop's wild Ideas. Sherman knew that his father had a gift for being able to convert Ideas into reality; Pop made things *happen*.

After a few minutes, Sherman said, "Can I ask a question?"

" 'May I... ' " Father corrected. "Ask away."

"Well, I was wondering... this is Rhoda's project. So how come you didn't ask her to come hunting tonight? It's real important to get the right materials, and she did do the design."

Father chuckled. "It is important. But I know I can trust you. So does your sister."

Sherman sighed. "I suppose. But she's been awfully cranky."

"I noticed. That's another reason I wanted you to come with me. You could use a change of scene."

"But why's she got to be that way?" Sherman wondered. "We try to be nice to her, but all she does is be crabby to us."

Father thought about this a moment before answering.

"It's a phase, Sherman," he finally said. "A phase of growing up. Suddenly your sister has all these huge Ideas and that's all she can think about. Remember last fall when you took a sudden interest in algebra and geometry? Whenever we had a math quiz, you always gave the answer before anyone else had a chance. That was kind of annoying for the other kids."

"Yeah, and I got scolded for it," the lad protested.

"You got *corrected*," Father said, "not scolded. And remember how Rhoda came to you afterwards and asked for help with her homework? She respects you, my boy. Now, I have a question for you."

"Okay!"

"What do you think of Rhodie's design?"

Sherman didn't have to think it over. "Excellent! I mean we studied the weight-to-lift ratios, the inflation-to-velocity quotient, and the loadings. It was Charlie's idea to use bamboo for the main elements. My brother is pretty clever," Sherman added, smiling.

"Yup," Father said, agreeing. "It runs in the family. So you approve of the design?"

"You bet. I mean there's all kinds of possible design configurations, depending on what we want it to do. But for a start, this looks good. You really ought to talk with Rhodie about it, though. She's the expert."

"Have you figured out a way to test it?"

Sherman made a gesture. "Sort of," he said. "Alignment... I guess you call it 'angle of attack'... is crucial with this kind of device. We're still working on that challenge." Sherman paused, then said, "Pop, my turn again, with another question."

Father had just finished the last pellet and was taking a final sip of tea. "Uh huh," he said, his powerful teeth gleaming in the darkness as a small crumb fell onto his dark shirt.

"How come we didn't get started on these adventures until Mom got the notion to get to the top of the cage wall?"

Once again, Father paused to consider the question and what its deeper meanings were.

"How come?" he repeated. "Hmmm-m-m. Let me explain how Creatures of our kind learn about life. You see, my boy," Father went on, "we all have certain lessons stored inside our bodies."

"Like in our chromosomes?"

"Inside our DNA. Listen, here's the Lesson about Ideas and Notions:

> *A seed will grow when the ground is ready.*
> *From that a tree will grow.*
> *You must tend the tree.*
> *When the fruit is ripe for picking,*
> *Be sure the tree is steady.*
> *And, uh, you are ready.*

That is from <u>Volume One</u> of the "*The Way of the Jungle.*"

Sherman looked over at his father, waiting for more. "Is that the end?" he finally asked.

"I think so."

"Gee, I'm sorry, Pop. I don't quite get it," Sherman admitted.

Father thought. Then he said, "Well, to tell you the truth, I don't, either. But I enjoy the cadence of our Lessons."

"Maybe there oughta be something about 'finger-licking' " Sherman offered. "To rhyme with 'picking'?"

"Good idea," Father said. "Let's head home. And no clicking."

"Or ticking."

"Enough with the jokes," Father said.

CHAPTER 12

THE IDEA COMES TO LIFE

Over the next nine days the air crackled with excitement in the Secret Workshop. Sometimes it is hard to appreciate how dynamic Guinea Pigs are, but when they get going on a project, a team of Oxen couldn't hold them back. Seriously.

Working whenever they had the chance, they were always carrying things: Tools, bamboo and titanium struts, ultra-strong fabrics, rolled-up plans, line, fasteners, parcels of food and drink, flashlights, and weapons. (Because an unfriendly Creature might sneak into the house some night—perhaps a Boa Constrictor or a Vampire Bat—the Fliffs decided to carry short swords [made from pins]. Just in case.)

Each night, each Team had an assignment: 'Collect a This or That', 'Sew along the line', 'Connect a strut to the control bar', and so on.

Quite often there were changes in Plans when the Chief Designer—Rhoda—found an error or a better way to solve a problem. Sometimes a Team had to go out three times in a night. All of this was hard work, and it had to be done right. But the Fliffs, like all Guinea Pigs, did their best work under the toughest conditions. As Father often reminded them, *"It is always cooler in the Jungle than it is in the fall."*

Nevertheless, for all the challenges and re-strictions of working at night and in total secrecy, the Fliffs completed their project on schedule.

The last stages of construction were the toughest, because the *machine* was pretty big. Its code name was *Moonseeker.*

The last stage of construction had to be done on the floor in Chloe's closet. When it was done, the Fliffs were bubbling with joy and eagerness to try it. But they didn't dare run a test until Chloe was safely not only out of her room, but out of the house. As it happened, Chloe was a popular girl and friends often invited her for sleep-overs. So it came to be, on a Tuesday night. When the Fliffs heard this, they decided to have the first ground test right away, at three-fifteen (3:15) in the morning. Naturally, it would be Rhoda who tried Moonseeker first.

At the Hour of the First Test, Rhoda's strong, healthy heart was bumping and pumping as she lifted the machine. Flexing her trim but strong sprinting muscles, Rhoda spun her sneakers (to heat them up) and took off at full speed across Chloe's floor.

She leaned forward and pushed, and leaned and pushed, gaining speed with every pounding step. Faster and faster the plucky Pig plunged across the moon-mottled wood floor, and harder she ran, and ran, and... and... had to stop before she hit the wall.

Nothing happened! Moonseeker seemed to be asleep.

Never one to quit, Rhoda spun around, took careful aim at the longest open part of the floor, and smoked her sneaks again. (A sneakers burn-out, you might say.) Bam, she was off like a gazelle, uncoiled and forcing every last ounce of power into a run that would make her machine, her creation, her DREAM, bring **glory** to the family Fliff.

Moonseeker uttered a few feeble flutters, but that was it. At the end of the test run, Rhoda's body was burning with fatigue. She lowered her machine to the floor. Gasping for breath and feeling the crush of defeat everywhere in her disappointed body, Rhoda stood and vowed .that she would not cry. As her father had said many times, when things had gone bad: *"A tear brings no flowers. Showers bring flowers."*

Unable to think beyond the sting of failure, Rhoda stood there, not knowing what to do. Then she felt a small paw slide inside hers.

"It wanted to go seeking, Rhodie," a tiny voice said. "It really did."

Rhoda couldn't speak, so she just hugged her sister. After a long, quiet moment it was Charlie who came to his big sister's side and took her other paw. "I got an idea," he said softly. "You want, I'll save it 'til tomorrow. Whatever you want, Rhodie."

Rhoda hugged him, too. She turned now, to see where Mom and Pop and Sherm were. Right there, side by side. Even in the dark, Rhoda could see brave smiles on their faces. Gleaming teeth.

When everything goes wrong, some Creatures want to crawl into bed and pull the covers over their head. Rhoda felt that way (except it would be shavings, not a blanket). But Mother had other ideas.

"Rhoda, dear, the Fliff family is not going to bed thinking about a test that was a little disappointing. Right, Fred?"

"Right as crispy carrots," Father declared cheerfully. "A family council meeting! We'll think of something!"

"Good," Mother said. "First, let's hide Moonseeker. Then back up to the cage and talk about what to do next. Does that sound fine to you, Rhoda?"

Rhoda shrugged. "Okay, Mom," she sighed. "I just hope all of you have some ideas."

By the time Moonseeker had been hidden and the Fliffs had elevatored back up to the cage, they were tired. They were ready, however, for a good discussion. Mother and Father let the children do most of the talking; they spoke up just to answer questions.

The family council meeting didn't take long. Remembering how nice Oyster and Charlie had been, Rhoda let them go first. Oyster, always the wild one, declared that Moonseeker had to go faster. When he heard that, Sherman clenched his fist in a triumphant gesture, saying "YESss!"

Charlie, always the 'Mister Go-Carefully', said Oyster was right but they needed a dummy to do a 'go faster' test that he had in mind.

Everyone laughed at *that* suggestion and Charlie had to explain that he meant a **dummy** dummy, not a particular Pig.

Rhoda asked Sherman what he thought.

Sherman grinned. "I think the little dummies... sorry, I meant to say little *kids*... are absolutely right, Rhodie. Go faster and use a dummy. Let's use Charlie's idea. And knowing Chaz, I bet he has an idea how to go faster! Right, Chaz?"

Charlie smiled a little and nodded.

Rhoda gave her brothers a Thumbs-up. Then she said to her parents, "If that's OK with you."

All four, tired but eager heads turned to the 'Higher Authorities'. This would be the really BIG test. If the parents said No, then everything was over. They would take Moonseeker apart, put the tools away, and just kind of... well, who knows? Just lump along 'til something interesting comes down the chimney.

Mother and Father looked at each other. The kids looked back and forth, wondering if the parents were exchanging secret signals. What was going to happen? Rhoda was bracing herself again for bad news. They all knew how she felt. The little kids were almost jumping up and down, they were so anxious.

"Yes," Mother and Father said together.

It took the kids a minute to realize that Rhodie's project was GO! They nearly shouted with joy.

"Tomorrow is a holiday," Mother said, "and all the Williams are going to see Matilda's aunt before she has her electric shock treatment. That means we will have the house to ourselves for about four hours. So, Rhoda, if you want to test Moonseeker, tomorrow would be a good time. Your decision."

Getting Moonseeker up to the cage turned out to be far more of an effort than expected. They hoisted the machine the long way, but found it impossible to move the top over the cage wall. Charlie had the solution, of course.

"Pull it up sideways, Sis, the long way across. You and Sherm can grab the ends and we'll get it the middle."

How great was that idea! All of a sudden, after a bit of struggling, Moonseeker was atop the cage wall. Rhoda was beside herself with excitement.

"Okay, Charlie," she said to her little brother, "let's hear your idea for what we should use for the dummy. We're ready any time you are."

Charlie nodded to his big sister. The lad had gained a ton of confidence in the last few days. "Gotcha," he said. "I'll go down and load the dummy in the Elevator. I'll stay down there to watch Moonseeker from below. All right?"

Rhoda hugged her brother. "Let Sherman help. And take swords," she said, reminding them about the new rule about self-defense.

Charlie grabbed two swords, nodded to his big brother, and both eager helpers hopped into the Elevator. Sherman operated the crank to lower the contraption. When they reached the floor of Chloe's room, both Fliffs turned and looked up.

Wow, there was Moonseeker, its pointed nose jutting way out past the edge of the cage. It sure was rad! Bright red, zoomy, and BIG. Rhoda and Pop were holding Moonseeker up, so the dummy could be fitted in the seat underneath it.

But as Sherm was staring up at the magnificent machine, all of a sudden he noticed something strange. Very strange. For some reason, Rhoda and Pop, and Mom and Oyster, were not looking at him. They were looking *across* the room, eyes wide and frightened, and they were trying to speak. W—H—A—T was going...

Sherman and Charlie spun around and looked toward Chloe's door. What they saw turned Pig knees to jelly.

There, crouching in Chloe's doorway—eyes blazing, fangs rasping, claws grasping, tail twitching, head low between its powerful shoulders, was the biggest, most terrifying

Creature they had ever seen! They knew instantly what and who it was. It was clever, hungry, tiger-striped Hunter the Cat. His alert ears were scarred from battle and his rippling muscles conveyed an aura of power and speed. The Cat's green-yellow slitted eyes sucked the very strength from his victims' legs. Hunter was in a Ready-to-Spring crouch, crawling and inching forward on coiled limbs that could rocket this powerful Cat a dozen feet into the air and across the room in two leaps.

Make no mistake, Hunter the Cat was smart. He had studied the Pigs from the darkness in the hallway. It would be an easy catch. Too easy, really. Planning his attack, Hunter figured if he merely pinned the helpless Guinea Pigs to the floor under one claw, and held them as bait, the other pathetic weak pigs in the cage would come down. Or if they didn't, no prob—he could get up into that silly cage in one leap. Hunter licked his chops and grinned maliciously. "ACTION TIME," Hunter growled to himself. He was quite pleased with himself.

Then two things happened, just as the cat was about to spring into action.

Sherman clutched his sword and in a wobbly voice, said, "Ch-Ch-Charlie, I-I-I'm g-g-gonna delay him. You RUN for the elevator, Charlie... Go Go GO!"

Charlie drew his sword, too, and stepped alongside his brother. He wanted to say 'We fight together, big brother' but his voice wouldn't work. The brothers bumped their shoulders together to signal that for better or worse, they were a team.

Hunter was surprised when he saw the ridiculous Creatures hold up those silly pointy things. Usually, Victim Creatures froze when they saw him coming, and Hunter had been counting on Pig Paralysis. Oh well, so what. They were small, slow, weak, and dumb and he was big, fast, powerful, and clever. (Handsome, too, so a few lady cats had said.) IT'S SHOW TIME, BIG GUY, he said to himself. YUM.

Well, maybe not, *Big Guy*. Did you happen to notice what those two dumb Victims were doing? Getting ready to fight, that's what. And those pointy *things*, Kitty Cat, are SWORDS! And did you notice that the *other* part of the Fliff Defense Team was mobilizing, too, Mister Green Eyes? Rhoda was lifting Moonseeker over her head. Hunter had ignited **PIG FURY!**

CHAPTER 13

THE RED BAT ATTACK

There are times in any Creature's life when suddenly, every-thing you know... <u>everything</u> that is important in your life... can change in the blink of an eye. Maybe the change will be good, maybe it will not be.

Some Creatures freeze when a huge change happens suddenly. They freeze, as Nature has taught them to do. (Think: Rabbits.) Other Creatures have been taught to just spin around and run like the Blue Blazes. (Squirrels.) Maybe they are fast enough to escape, maybe they are not.

Ah, then there are certain *very special* Creatures who understand *immediately... instantly...* that running would not help. Why not? Because they know that they can't run fast enough to escape. Therefore they must do something else. This is what the brain of a very special Creature (like a Guinea Pig) does: It figures out the *something else.*

Oh, they know the situation is terrible. But they *also* know that they will do the best they can and maybe, just maybe, what they do might allow them to escape OR it might create a diversion and allow a fellow Creature to escape.

(You should know that there are some Creatures, when they see that something strange has happened, just sit there and wait. For example, twenty-seven foot long Anacondas usually do not panic and run away. Nor do twenty-foot long Alligators. Dragons absolutely *love it* when something happens! Understand?)

Anyway, back to the absolutely horrible situation the Fliffs are in. There were Sherman and Charlie, on the floor of Chloe's room, and there was Hunter the Cat, also on the floor, about to enter Chloe's room. You know that GPs (Guinea Pigs) are small, and weak, and slow compared to Hunter Cat. Sherman and Charlie both knew this. They knew that trying to run from the terrible Cat would be an *exercise in futility*. And they also knew it would be futile to try to wrestle with the Cat and make him apologize and leave immediately with his tail between his legs. So, what could the two small Fliff lads do? Simply stand there, frightened but proud, and let the Cat take them? Just like that, give up? Goodbye family?

NO! The two brave lads looked at each other and nodded, no discussion necessary. They understood what had to be done. They made the choice. They would defend themselves. Chins out, shoulders back, fierce expressions on those round faces—they would defend themselves! They would hold on as long as they could, together, shoulder to shoulder, and maybe... who knows, maybe this act of courage would make the Cat forget about the others up there in the cage. Yes, Sherman and Charlie were going to help their families by distracting the Cat. That decision is called The Courage of Sacrifice.

Out came the swords. Again the brothers glanced quickly at each other, winked bravely, and CHARGED AT THE CAT! **"FLIFF ATTACK,"** they yelled together, and began to run at Hunter.

At the exact same moment, Rhoda saw what was happening and understood what her brothers were doing. Oh, my, how much she admired her brothers' courage. What brave little guys they are, she thought. But, she sobbed to herself, you guys are no match for a mighty Cat like that, not by yourselves. She had to do something, something smart and fast and right now! There was only one thing she could do. Only one. It was now or never.

Rhoda and Sherm had done all their research, all the calculations, all the careful design and construction. Darn it, Moonseeker should fly. It should. But the trial runs on Chloe's floor had failed miserably. Rhoda had run as fast as she could, but the machine just would not fly.

Later the other night when they had talked about the failure, Charlie suggested that the *reason* for the failure was that the wing had not gone *fast* enough. Was he right? Well, there was only one way to find out. Rhoda lifted Moonseeker way up over her head. She shook it to loosen the wing fabric. Then, teeth bared and growling, she began sprinting along the top of the cage wall as fast as her strong, tan legs could go.

Mother and Father saw everything, too. Their two sons were in ultra serious danger... and now Rhoda was at risk, too! Should they stay in the cage and protect Oyster? That wouldn't accomplish *anything.* The Fliffs knew that Hunter could leap from the floor to the cage, and the three of them were no match for the Cat.

What to do, what to do? The heavy responsibility of being parents. But in two seconds they knew what to do. Betsy and Fred looked at each other. The expression they shared was of greatest love and trust... and reality. Sometimes you may not be doing the best thing, but if you must do something, do the absolute best you can. Always!

GO, RHODIE, GO! they yelled together, as they saw the pilot and her mighty red wing, Moonseeker, leap off the end of the cage wall and turn its nose DOWNWARDS. Before it disappeared from view they heard the great wing go **POP** as it filled with air and began to carry, actually carry, the brave child in her diving attack.

Father grabbed a sword. *"Betsy,"* he shouted, *"get a sword and protect Oyster and yourself. Please, dear."* Without another word, he jammed a grappling hook on the top of the cage wall and over he went, rappelling down like the experts he had seen on TV.

"FLIFF POWER!" Rhoda shrieked, as the nose of the flying wing rocketed toward the huge Cat. She worked the Control bar harder, to *drop* Moonseeker's nose and make it go faster. Twisting her sleek brown body a smidge, she corrected direction and aimed at the Cat's fierce fangs! Sherman and Charlie heard the loud POP and in that instant Moonseeker zoomed over their heads, Rhoda yelling for all her worth. **"FLIFF POWER,"** they all yelled. All three warriors hit Hunter at the same time.

The Fliff defenders hit the Cat easily, because he had been... get this... FROZEN! For the first time in his life he had seen something so utterly weird he couldn't move. He was frozen with fear! These dopey little Creatures had suddenly turned into fearsome warriors and a gigantic red bat had come screaming out of the sky.

Hunter managed to duck his head a little, but Moonseeker gave him a mighty whack and as he was rearing up to flee, sharp pains hit him in the knees. As his feet spun to run, he heard another yell and THREE MORE WARRIORS were roaring across the floor.

Too Much. WAY too much! Hunter spun around and leapt through the open door, into the hallway and down the stairs. He went so fast his feet only touched one stair. He FLEW out the open front door and before you could say Celery Stalks he was gone.

Such whooping and hollering!

Rhoda was so thrilled that Moonseeker had actually flown, she did three cartwheels and then ran to embrace her brave brothers. Oyster was being hugged by her father for being brave and when Mother joined the party she just pulled the entire family together so she could touch all of them and see that they were all safe. Moonseeker lay on the floor, its proud sailwing now empty of air. But the beautiful red flying machine still had a very purposeful look to it. So did the swords. They were carefully stacked against Moonseeker. Father detached himself from the group and grabbed a sword. He caught Sherman's attention and signaled for the lad to follow him.

"Where are we going, Pop?"

"The front door. I can feel a draft of cold air. I think someone left the door partly open, so we'd better close it before Hunter... well, you know."

Sherman shivered. "He's gone away for good, hasn't he?"

Father slowly shook his head. "He'll be back," he said, in an odd way. "Maybe not now, maybe not tomorrow, but someday. Let's go."

The children were still excited when they all got back in the cage. Moonseeker had been hidden in the closet, the Elevator was in the hidden drawer under the table, and the climbing lines and ladder were concealed under the shavings. The children were all talking at once, about the expression on Hunter's face, about how wonderful Moonseeker was, and about being scared.

Mother and Father let them carry on. It was nice to see the kids so enthusiastic and so appreciative of each other. Sherm and Chaz had bonded much more, now that they had gone to battle together. In turn, everyone was thrilled that Rhodie had bravely launched herself and Moonseeker at the dreadful Cat. And of course, all the other kids praised Oyster for pitching in **again.** (Remember how she was going to rescue her family from the dreadful ROBOT?)

But then someone, probably Sherman, noticed that Mother and Father had been talking quietly and now were quiet. Then the rest of the kids noticed. "Is anything wrong?" Rhoda asked.

Mother glanced at Father. It was a look the children knew well. Silence suddenly fell over the Fliff family. Yup, something was...

"Not *wrong*," Father said. "Serious." Father took a deep breath. "Your mom and I are very proud of you. All of you. And we both agree that we've had some great adventures."

The children's faces fell. Hearing the words *serious* and *had great adventures* sure sounded like the end.

"But this is going too fast. Hunter's arrival proved that. We simply don't have enough experience to know all the things that can go wrong. Maybe it isn't possible to know every-thing..."

"But we should know more," Mother filled in.

"We should... we *have* to know more!" Father declared. "Moonseeker is a fabulous machine. The problem is..." he looked at Rhoda and saw how sad she looked. Rhoda knew what was coming "...the problem is," he repeated, "we can't fly it in the house. There's not enough room and we don't dare get caught. Also, Hunter knows about us now, and believe me, they don't call him Hunter for nothing. He will be back."

Father looked at Sherman now. "Son, the Elevator works great, and I'd love to go Outside. We all would. But let's face it—we are Jungle Creatures. Jungles are warm. We would freeze Outside here." Father shrugged. "So, unless or until someone has a magical Idea about how our kind of Creature can endure the cold, Mom and I agree that we are sticking close to home. Basically, that means Chloe's room until further notice. I'm sorry, kids." He was, too.

All the Fliffs were sorry, especially after the big victory celebration for Moonseeker's flight AND scaring Hunter away. They all wondered: Is this all there is? Have we reached the limit of Pig Power? A collective sadness fell over the Fliffs like a blanket made heavy by tears. Like a face turned downwards by sadness.

Then, trying to think of any little word that might lift their spirits, Father remembered a wise saying from the Book of the Jungle. It had never failed to make him feel better. "Cheer up," he said. "It is always darkest before it gets light in the morning."

"Before dawn," Mother whispered to him.

Then Oyster piped up: "Where there's a way we will, um, go there. I think."

No one else said anything. No one could, because they were all choked up.

CHAPTER 14

THE (Secret) WORKSHOP

"You were carrying *what*?" Charlie asked a second time. Oyster had explained it once, but Charlie still couldn't believe his ears.

"You already *know*," Oyster said. " 'cause I already told you *twice!*" Oyster was getting peeved because she had a pretty good idea he was laughing at her.

"You attacked... you attacked Hunter... with a **toothpick?** " Charlie said, laughing so hard that he fell over and lay on his back in the shavings, kicking his feet in the air.

It was next morning after the Hunter Episode, the house was quiet, and the Fliffs were getting over their sadness about having to put away Moonseeker and maybe stop their adventures. The laughter they were enjoying (except for Oyster) was really a kind of relief. Last night had nearly ended as a total disaster for the Fliff family. Bravery and quick thinking had saved them, but a lot of good luck, too.

After breakfast and math lessons, while the children were straightening up the cage, they had been telling stories about last night's adventure. They described Oyster ferociously galloping across Chloe's floor to go after Hunter. What had gotten everyone laughing hysterically was that Oyster had joined the Attack Team *armed with a toothpick.*

Charlie, who had seen the others carrying swords, could not imagine why Oyster would go after a Cat when all she had to protect herself was a wood toothpick. Really curious, he had asked Oyster why.

And Oyster, the honest child, had replied, "Well, you know, Charlie, I was so scairt I grabbed my sword 'cept it wasn't and I didn't notice what I was holding and I was running after that HUGE Cat and I wanted to save you and Sherm and... well, you know..."

That was when Rhoda spoke up. "Chaz, you and Sherm were brave to go after the Cat. Just don't you forget that your sister was brave, too. She was brave twice, as a matter of fact. Remember who was going to attack the Robot when she thought it was attacking us? Okay, let's finish our work here." Rhoda winked at Oyster, who really felt proud.

So the children completed their chores. The rest of the day rolled along all right. A few games, naps, snacks... the usual things. You know. Ho hum.

But their lives had changed, just as Father knew would happen. The Fliffs had tasted freedom and adventure... and fear. Change did not open onto Easy Street. Change opened the door to Adventure, to Ideas, but to Danger, too. Father wondered what parents should do, when Changes and Dangers happen to the family? Say NO to everything?

Last night, when everyone else was asleep, Father knew he had to do some more thinking. Just as Betsy had felt an urge to 'get around', he had to understand the importance of Change in a Guinea Pig's life. In a serious matter like this, all Father had to guide him was what his ancestors had figured out a long time ago. The Wise Ones. Father thought of the Jungle Rules and what would apply to him and his family.

<u>First</u>, Guinea Pigs had learned to live in the Jungle. That meant they were clever, and being clever meant having Ideas.

<u>Second</u>, GPs come up with good *Bold* Ideas.

<u>Third</u>, if you have Bold Ideas, you also have a choice: <u>Dreaming</u> about the Bold Ideas or actually <u>Doing</u> them.

<u>Fourth,</u> Ideas are food for the spirit.

<u>Fifth</u>, Always plan ahead and carry extra food with you.

<u>Sixth</u>, Change for the sake of change is like a sword made from lightning. (Fred wasn't sure what this meant, but it sounded like a Basic Truth.)

He fell asleep listening to the Midnight Special, a night train that carried cords of wood to a sawmill in a faraway place called Mobile. It made a good sound, that train did.

Then Father did something completely strange. He got up, quietly took a climbing line from under the shavings, and let himself out of the cage and down to the floor. He needed to learn something, something new, and for some peculiar reason he had to do it right this minute. Maybe it was the sound of the train in the cold winter night.

The Secret Workshop had been moved into Chloe's closet, because it was bigger. It was warm in there. Safe, too. It was very unlikely that anyone would discover the loose baseboard and hidden latch.

Often, when Father worked in the shop, he would take a break to explore the surroundings. The old Victorian farmhouse had plenty of spaces behind the walls, especially around closets and chimneys. Exploring these places would *not* be a good idea *unless* they had a light to show the way in the darkness. Lights they did have, and lots of them—small flashlights of all sizes and types. Chloe's mother worked in a place that did light manufacturing, and she collected samples for testing. Some of these lights were small, very bright, and perfect for exploring.

So that was how Father had found a passageway that went from the closet, around a wooden enclosure, directly to a small hole that opened onto the balcony. Father had made a crude cover to conceal the hole and keep the winter winds out. Tonight, he decided to go through the hole and stand on the balcony. Why he felt the urge to go out there, he didn't know, but he did.

Although it was bitter cold on the balcony, and way up above the lawn, Father felt a thrill as he stood in the OPEN AIR. There was a half-moon settling in the sky. The half-disk was a brilliant silver color, with a golden tinge. Looking closely, Father could just discern the other half of the moon, the half that was in shadow. It was a bit eerie. Father thought he had never seen anything as majestic as that distant, cold beacon.

Father shivered. He heard the bitter cold wind, and felt it all over his muscular body, but he stood on tiptoes and peered between the spindles of the railing and saw the silvery blanket of shiny snow that went across the lawn on out into the field. Farther out, the field fell off steeply. Bert and Chloe called that area Big Hill. They went sliding on Big Hill. Father could not see Big Hill, but the stories they told sounded so exciting! He wanted to be sliding on the icy snow, sliding faster and faster. Father could feel the speed and hear the cold wind whistling past his ears. If only he could go...

But the Dream Wish had to be stopped. Father was shivering already and he had to get back inside before he turned into a furry icicle. Even as he scurried around beams and corners, Father knew that there just *had to be* another Adventure for the Fliffs. It didn't seem right that they had learned how to get in and out of the cage, and explore, and go trapezing and build Elevators and Moonseeker... and then stop. Guinea Pigs were an ancient and proud line of Creatures. They had been given the Gift of making Ideas! There *had* to be a way. The Outdoors had called him, had called all of them.

Back in the Workshop, as Father rubbed his chilly paws together, he heard the call of the Outdoors again, and it was clear as a bell and *this* time he knew what the Plan was. *Exactly* what the Plan was. The Plan... an Idea. A Challenge. Oh Pigger-oo, what an Idea! Tomorrow he would begin work. In an instant, in a flash, Father knew how to do it.

He could see a picture of the Plan in his head. He knew what he wanted to do, and maybe how to do it. But the big question was: How could they stay warm Outdoors? If they couldn't stay warm, the Idea would never see the light of day. Father frowned as he warmed his paws and thought about the Project. Hmmm, maybe Betsy would have an Idea. As long as it didn't involve dancing.

A half-hour later, back home and warm in bed, Father heard his family in their sleep, all safe and sound. He was so excited he wanted to awaken them and shout Hey, Everyone, it's Change time! We'll need a Retriever. Yup, and a faster Elevator. Warmers, and of course... ZEBRA, HERE WE COME!

And there you are, dear friends. You have just learned how a Guinea Pig thinks and how it comes up with fabulous Ideas. However, we do have to wonder, don't we: Can Fred Fliff actually, you know, make something for Outdoors? For Getting Around? In the bitter COLD?

Oh, probably not. Probably it was simply a cuckoo Idea that sounded neat at the moment but would fizzle under the weight of reality.

CHAPTER 15

ELEVATOR DANGER

Rhoda stopped. She grasped the Elevator crank handle and held her breath. She froze every muscle in her well-toned body and listened.

There it was again. A Tap... pause... a Bump... then a Tap and a Bump...

Although warmly dressed against the winter wind and cold, Rhoda shivered. She knew what the Tap and Bump sound was. Bad news. Then, over the sound of the freezing wind, she heard the desperate call of her brother. He sounded a million miles away...

"**R..hod... ie**," he called, with real urgency in his voice. "Crank me up!"

Rhoda tried. The crank wouldn't turn. *The Elevator was jammed.*

"Sherman," she whispered frantically, "wait. I heard something. Don't make a sound."

She didn't have to warn him. Sherman had heard the sound, too.

Rhoda stepped away from the Elevator mechanism and leaned over the railing. Oh Oh! Looking up at her was Sherm, eyes begging her to do something. He was hanging on to the Elevator line and swinging in the wind and it might as well have been broad daylight, because...

Sherm was suspended right in front of the Williams' living room window—in the bright light that was bursting from the room. All anyone had to do was look out the window and there'd he be, plain as day. Sherman Fliff, Guinea Pig adventurer, dressed in a black snow suit, swinging in front of the house window, at night, as if he didn't

have a care in the world. Disaster had struck...
AGAIN!

It always mystified Father how innocently these things began. The conversation had gone something like this, he remembered:

"We could never go out, Betsy, not for long, anyway. We'd freeze."

And Betsy saying, "Oh, really? Suppose we had warm clothes?"

And him saying, "Oh sure. What, we'd wear Chloe's socks? Bert's gloves?" Then being annoyed because Mother seemed to be laughing at him.

And then, *next night*, he and Sherman are conducting another search in the dark house, wondering if the dratted Cat had gotten in and double-wondering if they could find the fabric Betsy wanted.

But lo and behold, *four nights later*, as if by magic, but really by hard work, all six Fliffs had Outdoor suits that were warm and very attractively tailored. Plus, they had boots and gloves—boots borrowed from abandoned action figure toys, and gloves skillfully made from the super-insulating fabric the suits were made from. Ingenious! So *that* was what Mother had been laughing at. She'd been working on the suits!

Naturally, after having tested the snow suits by staying out on the balcony for an hour, Sherman decided he had to build a better Elevator and, just in case, a Retriever. The Spirit of Adventure had swept over the entire Fliff family.

Later, however, as an excited Fliff family got ready for bed, Mother brought up the subject they had been avoiding. "Everyone," she said in a soft voice that sounded a little sad, "I know what fun we had out there on the balcony, with the suit being so toasty warm, but I have to remind all of you that we have a huge problem. It's Hunter and those other dangers we don't have any experience with. Sherman, I know you want to try out your Elevator. And Rhoda, that beautiful Moonseeker is just itching to be flown Outdoors. However, have any of you actually looked *down* and seen how far away the ground is? We might as well be on top of a mountain! Before we do any more stunts, you'll have to convince me that we know what we're doing!" She looked over at Father, who looked uncomfortable.

"I don't imagine Hunter goes around Outside," Rhoda protested. "It's cold and slippery on the snow."

"But he came here," Sherman said. "To this house. He doesn't live here. He was outside and he was hunting."

"Oh, hey," Oyster piped up suddenly, all smiles, "maybe we don't hafta worry. He's gonna be all cured soon."

Everyone stared at her, wondering what she had gotten mixed up about, this time.

"Well," Oyster said defensively, "you don't haffa look at me that way. I heard Missus Williams talking on the phone to Hunter's mother... you know what I mean... not the *Cat* who's his mother, it was the woman who..."

"We get it," Father said. "What did they say?"

Oyster scratched her head. "Well, uh, Missus Williams said 'Why's he going to the vet, Martha?' whatever a vet is, and then Martha musta said something, and then Missus Williams said, " 'Oh, he's gonna be fixed? That will be nice.' So, see? Maybe if he's fixed up, we don't have to worry."

Father shook his head slowly and shrugged. "Maybe, maybe not," he said. "But for sure, he will not be in a great mood. I think we must continue with the plan to get the Sun Bombs. Plus the swords, and I like your idea of the Ghost, Oyster. We can do that, too. Plus, don't forget we have the Pig Alert."

And of course everyone was eager to try out the new and improved Elevator. Especially since they could go Outside and keep warm now. Sherman, the designer, claimed the job of taking the first ride. 'Well, why not, son, what could go wrong. The first Elevator worked like a charm. This one will, too. I know it will.'

That's how stuff happens. Innocently.

While Mother, Father, and Oyster began pulling the Elevator line—which was very hard to do, because they couldn't get a good grip on it—Charlie and Rhoda were struggling with the Elevator cranking mechanism.

"B... ang... it!"

"I heard Sherman say that," Charlie said to his sister. "Sherm said to bang it. Watch out." Using the flat of a small but strong gloved paw, Charles gave the locking ratchet a good swat. Something clicked. "Go ahead, Rhodie, see if that did it." So saying, Charlie stuck his head over the railing just in time to see a flood of bright light slash across the lawn. Someone had opened the back door!

"CRANK!" Charlie whispered sharply to his sister.

She did, and as Charlie watched, Sherman began to rise. Up and up...

A dark shadow moved into the splash of indoor light that had flooded a segment of snowy back yard. Someone was coming out!

"Another foot," Charlie whispered sharply. "Then stop!"

Charlie watched in horror as none other than Mr. Williams himself walked out onto the snow, shining a flashlight along the foundation UNDER the window, then around the yard. He looked in the rose bushes, in the cellar windows, everywhere but up.

"NOTHING," he called, to someone inside the house.

Sherman had a bird's eye view of all the excitement. He was exactly one inch above the lighted window, in shadow. He was still as a Mouse at a Cat Convention.

A quarter-hour later the lights went out in the living room, and an hour later the house was quiet... as much as an old house was willing to hush its aches and pains. When he was sure the People were in bed and asleep, Sherman gave the signal, the secret Pig Whistle, and little by little Rhoda and Charlie were able to haul Sherman back up to the balcony. What a relief that was!

Sherman thanked his brother and sister for the rescue and then told Charlie to head back in and go to bed... quietly. He said that he and Rhodie had a little work to finish up, and then they'd go back inside, too. Charlie, who was tired out, agreed.

When Charlie was gone, Rhoda asked her brother what *that* had been all about.

"I have to prove we can get down from the balcony, Rhodie. And I was the one who built the new Elevator. If you aren't too tired..." He paused. Sherman knew she would *never* admit to being

97

tired if he was going to stay up. "...we can give the Elevator another try," he said.

Of course Rhoda wasn't tired.

It didn't take long for Sherman to make a small adjustment in the cranking mechanism. They carefully re-wound the line and the Elevator was all ready to try again. Sherman stepped into the sling. "All set?" he asked his sister.

"I suppose," she replied.

"What's wrong?" he asked.

"Well, I sort of... I guess I feel kind of guilty, Sherman. Staying out here by ourselves, without permission. Maybe it isn't right."

Sherman sighed. "Look, Rhoda, isn't it kind of late in the game to feel guilty? We've been out here for an hour, for gosh sake. Besides, we did get permission."

"What are you talking about, Sherman?"

"When Mom and Pop and the kids went back inside, Pop whispered to be careful."

"What?" Rhoda blurted. "They know?"

"Of course, Rhodie. They know everything. Lower me down, sis."

Without further ado, Rhoda did just that. The cranking mechanism worked just fine on the new device and before you could say Fresh Carrots, Sherman Fliff was standing on the ground. He was OUTSIDE!

It was the first time he had ever been Outside. Everything was so totally different. The hard-crusted snow made funny crunchy noises and Sherman could feel the wind frisking around his Snow Suit and nipping at his nose. Above, looking up and up and up, he saw a sky more enormous than he ever could have imagined. Sherman saw the stars and planets twinkling so brightly. He knew how far away they were, from his astronomy lessons, and it thrilled him to realize that he was seeing light, which was photons, from objects that were billions of miles away.

Around the back yard there was a conglomeration of trees and bushes, of hills and bumps, and of shadows and shimmery ice surfaces. Just beyond where the last bush was, lay a flat area and the crest of Big Hill. From Chloe's window Sherman had seen part of the Hill and how far away the pond and woods were. The entire scale of this new world was dizzying.

Sherman felt as if... as if he was a part of Everything. He opened his arms to embrace the gorgeous and mysterious Universe. Sherman had discovered another World. Other Worlds!

But, as reality in this world actually behaves, two nights later the World turned out to be not quite as welcoming as the Fliffs had hoped. The Fliffs would need all the Courage, Luck, and Inventions they could get their trembling paws on.

CHAPTER 16

A NEW JUNGLE

The night had been ferociously wild. Between midnight and dawn, howling winds drove great mounds of snow across roads and fields and tiny snow crystals into cracks and crevices. Because of crazy drifting, the snow was piled five feet deep in valleys and elsewhere the cold, bare ground was scoured clean.

A small pyramid of fine snow had piled up *inside* the house, on the sill of Chloe's North window. Now and then a mass of snow would slide off the slate roof and crash to the ground. The wind sounded like a strange animal. It was not fit out there for man nor beast.

The morning brought no improvement. Sleet had replaced the snow, and wind threw the small, sharp crystals against the house. When sleet hit the windows, one might fear the glass would break.

Then, by night, the storm front was gone, replaced by dropping temperatures. When Bert and Chloe walked on the icy crust in back of the house, the Fliffs could hear their footsteps... Crunch, crunch, crunch, the sound of Winter cereal.

Were the Fliffs discouraged? Would the fierce weather put a crimp in their plans? They couldn't have been happier. **They loved it!** By night fall, the sky had cleared, the wind had gone, and judging by the draughts inside, it had turned very cold. Perfect conditions for their first big Family Expedition OUTSIDE.

Why were the Fliffs so excited about this night? Because—they thought—**the conditions were absolutely awful for a Cat**. (Luckily, the Fliffs didn't know about Coyotes, Lynx, Fox, Wolves, Mink, Weasels, Bears, Marten, Fisher Cats, Catamount, and Feral Dogs. Or Great Snowy Owls. However, the Fliffs <u>did</u> know how to avoid giant Creatures like *Tyrannosaurus rex*. Want to know how? It's easy. When you hear *T. rex* tromping across the crusty snow, hide. Just be sure NOT to hide where *T. rex* is going to put his foot down.)

So, when they heard the *Midnight Special* coming around the bend, the Fliffs were up, out of the cage, into the Secret Workshop, and all suited up for bitter cold. They did all that in five minutes flat. Four minutes later they were on the balcony, with Sherman's new Elevator hooked up, as well as his also-new Retriever Line, just in case. They gathered together for last-minute instructions.

"You don't mind staying on the balcony, Charles?" Mother asked.

Charles shook his head. "No, Mom. I practiced with the Retriever, Sherm and me and..."

" 'Sherm and *I* .' "

"Right. Sorry. I know how to work the brake and I'm strong enough to wind up the spring. I'll go next time."

"Good lad," Father said. "Okay, then. Rhoda, you carry the Ghost and Whistlers."

He got a Thumbs up.

"Sherman, you have the Sun Bomb." Check.

"Swords." Five Thumbs up.

"I have the safety line and another Sun Bomb," Father said. "Last reminder: I know we aren't worried about Hunter in the snow. Still, we must be careful out there. If anyone... I mean **anyone**... sees or hears something odd, give the **PAW**: the **P**ig **A**lert **W**histle and we go into Defensive Mode. Right?"

Five thumbs up.

In a flash, one by one, the Explorers stepped through the railing onto the Elevator sling and down they went. In seven seconds they were on the ground. For the first time ever, the Fliff family (minus Charlie) was Outside together, in the New Jungle. It was stupendously glorious... and cold.

The Fliffs held hands and formed a line. They moved their feet back and forth to feel the crust. They took deep breaths to see if the cold could hurt. (No. Well, a little.) And then they looked around at the yard, at the trees and bushes, and finally up at the huge sky all dotted with stars. At that very moment a meteor crashed into the upper atmosphere and burned in a brilliant slash of light and smoke.

"Awe... some!" Rhoda exclaimed. She knew exactly what it was. "I made a wish. I can't tell you what it was, but one word is..."

Everyone looked at her.

Rhoda spelled it. "F. U. N." She laughed.

That got them going. They turned and looked up at the balcony, to be sure Charlie was okay. He waved. They also saw that all the lights were out in the house. All right! It was EXPLORE TIME!

The Fliffs began to cross the big lawn on the frozen crust. They would go ten feet and stop and listen, move and stop, move and stop, practicing the **NAW**, the **N**ight **A**lert **W**alk. Before long they had a nice rhythm to the **W**alk, so they continued in a direction that seemed to draw them like a magnet. They were heading directly to a place they had seen a hundred times from the window in Chloe's room. B*ig Hill.*

It is common, in exploration of desert or jungle, ocean, or back yard, for explorers to move along much faster than they think they're going. Before you could say *Carrots!* the explorers were on the brink of the Hill. The horizon seemed to open up and expand all the way into the night sky. It was like being at the edge of the world!

The Fliffs managed to utter a long, hushed "O..H..H..h..h... hhh."

Finally, Mother spoke. "Goodness, isn't this breath-taking. I thank all of you for being so inventive and brave." She patted Oyster's hood, then turned to Father. "Time to get home, don't you think, dear? Charles will begin to worry."

Father looked back at the house. Because of the brush and hill, all he could see was the roof. The house was pretty far away.

"Hmm, I guess you're right."

"What say, Sherm," Oyster said to her brother, "want to race?"

Father laughed. "Not tonight, kiddos. We will follow the same procedure we used to get here—**FAW**..."

"**FAW**?" Sherman said.

"What?" Father said.

"**SAW**," Oyster piped up. "**S**tep, uh, **A**lways, **W**ISELY!" She was so proud of herself for remembering.

"Oh for gosh sa..." Father stopped and froze in his tracks.

Everyone stopped.

Father gave the Pig Danger Signal: Z... z....z....z... **zzzz**..t... t.

Everyone was motionless.

"Up there, by that large rock," he whispered in the Ultra-High Frequency that only Guinea Pigs and Bats can hear. "I thought... I saw something... Duck... down. Watch... by... the rock. Slowly, get the Ghost out. And the Sun Bombs. When I say 'Move'... slide left behind that little hillock."

Down they went, and over, in the shelter of a shallow hill. The Protective Devices were readied. Everyone scanned the area by looking back and forth slowly. Then Rhoda saw something. She nudged her brother and whispered in his ear. "Short tree... right of rock. Like a piece of rope... Pass the message."

The message was passed. They watched.

And saw the piece of rope... *twitch*. A trick of the eye? No! Another *twitch*, and another. No doubt now—some creature was lurking behind the low brush between the tree and the rock. Father gathered his family close, so they could communicate extra softly. "It knows we're here," he said, careful not to sound frightened.

"That's reassuring, Fred," Mother said.

"You bet," Father said. "Everyone warm?"

Yeses.

"Good. We'll wait."

In the shadow of the tree, the Creature was waiting, too. He was not cold, but he wasn't toasty warm, either. He was definitely impatient and he definitely knew that the Little Things had seen him. They were small and they had strange signals. Not like anything he'd seen or heard before... Wait! Wait a minute...

Of course! He recognized who they were. Those accursed little monsters inside the house! What were they doing out here? And where was

that awful flying Red Bat? Angry now, Hunter
snarled and flexed his sharp claws on a rock. If
their Flying Protector Creature wasn't with
them—maybe it only lived in the house—this
would be the best time to get his revenge!

'I shall attack,' Hunter decided. He flexed
his long muscles and his tail twitched again. His
brain calculated the distance and timing for a
spring, a sprint, and a leap. Tensing and aiming
where he had last seen them, Hunter gathered his
powerful muscles into springing position...

Then Hunter the Cat had a rare moment of
doubt. Now he couldn't see any of them. Maybe
those foolish creatures have run. They could have
run, the cowardly little things. Tensing his
muscles and ready to attack the spot where he
had *last* seen the little cowards, Hunter narrowed
his green and yellow eyes to examine the target

area. He noticed something odd. Something very odd.

Rising slowly out of the snow was an ugly white thing, a shapeless white blob that was like nothing he had ever seen before. And it was making an awful sound, a sound like... savage Bats. Hunter could tell that this strange white thing was not afraid. Good, he told himself, as he worked to pump up his courage. This is a challenge! I can conquer any challenge!

What... WHAT?

The noise got louder and the thing grew arms, and on the arms were shiny eyes. Hunter blinked and squeezed his own eyes, to be sure what he was seeing was real. It was real... it was *terrible*. It was a sickening nasty *Snow Creature*. The situation had changed. Now Hunter knew he was going to have a wicked tough battle with this thing. 'Alright', he said to himself, to prop up his courage, 'you want a battle, you got one!'

As Hunter rose, slowly this time, to show how big he was, the Creature screamed at him and suddenly the world EXPLODED. A blast of FIERCE LIGHT hit Hunter's eyes. His head filled with swirling suns. His brain went limp. His legs wobbled. Unable to see anything except a hurricane of blinding light, and deafened by the crazy noise, Hunter knew deep in his belly that he was cooked. Done for. Annihilated. Doomed. Obliterated. The Creature would destroy him with strange and powerful weapons. Only one thing left to do.

Hunter the Cat spun around and jumped as hard as he could, to get as far away as he could, as quickly as he could. He took one huge, mighty, high, lunging leap... and—*unable to see anything*—he rammed headfirst right into a tree trunk. **BANG!**

Hunter was out for the count. Lights-Outville.

Seeing this, the Fliffs were overjoyed. They nearly cheered, and would have, except for Pig Training. The Cat had knocked himself out. But they knew they had only a few seconds to get back to the house before Hunter came to. Holding on to their powerful flashlights and swords, they made fast tracks home.

When all of them got safely onto the balcony, huffing and puffing, Charlie said quite loudly, "I betcha you had *fun*, am I right? No kidding, am I right?"

Mother pointed to Sherman. "You tell Charlie all about it," she said.

Sherman did, all the while hoping that the story of another close call with the Cat wouldn't convince his brother to stay home from now on. Then Sherm thought: Maybe we all oughta stay home. That's the new Jungle Pop talks about? Wow.

CHAPTER 17

The Strange Little Creature
With the Tin Can Shell

"I hope you're sure about this, Pop."

"That sure makes two of us, son. Believe me. When I say **'Go'** just push me over."

'Yeah, push and *hope*,' Sherman said to himself. He waited until his father was inside the can... which nearly tipped over while Pop was climbing in... and had given the signal.

"Go," said a small, tinny voice.

Sherman closed his eyes, breathed a deep sigh of double *Hope*, and pushed the tin can. As it tipped, a thousand questions sped through Sherman's head:

Was the line strong enough?

Was the Elevator strong enough?

What about the handle on the tin can?

Suppose the trap door opened and Pop fell out?

Suppose Thunder woke up in a really bad mood?

Well, too late for questions now. Off the tree branch went the tin can, with Pop inside, plummeting like a rock. Seeing the tin can fall, Sherman thought that no matter how long he lived, he would never, ever see another stunt as crazy as this one. And it hadn't been Oyster's idea, either. Nope, it was Pop's, all the way.

All the way was from the branch almost to the ground, just in front of Thunder's door. And still attached to the line, if you please.

The way *it*—this crazy stunt Pop was doing—started was like this...

The unexpected *second* encounter with Hunter had left the Fliffs all shook up and extremely grateful to be back home in one piece. Now they got the picture that Hunter was very dangerous.

Second, they had made a **big** mistake by assuming the Cat would *not* be out on a cold night. And third, although no one said this aloud, the Fliffs knew how vulnerable they were Outside. Oh sure, they had invented a few tricks, like the flash bulb Sun Bombs and the electronic whistle, but hunters like Hunter wouldn't be fooled the next time around. Of course, once they were inside and settled down, they had to tell Charlie about the Great Escape. That was all Charlie needed to hear. What, outside—in the freezing cold—with a huge Cat waiting to pounce? I don't think so, Charlie said to himself. Not *this* Pig, thank you very much.

So, yet again, the Fliffs went to bed late and tired. Very tired. But an hour later Father was still awake and he could hear Sherman tossing and turning, trying to go to sleep. Finally, Father tapped Sherman on the shoulder and gestured for the boy to follow him. Father made a Sh-h-h-h sign. Together they put the ladder up to the top of the wall, hooked the climbing lines to the wood, and slid down the lines to the floor.

When they were comfortably settled under the table, Sherman whispered, "What's up, Pop? Thinking about the Cat?"

"In a way," his father said reflectively. "What the problem is, Sherman, it is *more* than the problem with the Cat. It's about getting around, and Ideas, and all the exciting things we've been doing. I mean, over there in the closet," Father pointed to his left, "hidden under some old rags, is Moonseeker. I still can't believe how great it looks."

"Wicked," Sherman said.

"Wicked indeed. And the clever Elevator you built, and that great Retriever we haven't even tried out yet. We are Guinea Pigs, son. Our roots are from the Jungle and our hearts are from... uh... from... wait... uh..."

"The moon?" Sherman suggested.

Father shrugged. "Sure, why not. The point is, Sherman, we need help Outside. We need protection. Your Sun Bomb saved us tonight, but suppose Hunter wears sunglasses next time. Suppose he shuts his eyes. So, we have a choice: We can give up exploring Outside or find a safer way to explore. I have an Idea that might work. Want to hear it?"

Of course Sherman did, and Father proceeded to explain what he had been thinking about. Sherman listened carefully. Then he asked questions, to be sure he understood the Idea. He asked more questions and got more answers. Then he asked a third set of questions and this time Father only had vague answers. When Sherman persisted, Father finally said *Don't worry, it will all work out just fine*. That was when Sherman had his *first* doubt about the Idea.

The *second* doubt was when they made the long trip across two big yards, at night, lugging the Elevator, Pop's Safety Cage, a bunch of line, two swords, and two Sun Bombs. Sherman kept looking around for any sign of Hunter. He also wished they had a Mule or some big Creature to carry all the stuff.

Sherman's *third* doubt arrived when they finally got to Thunder's dog house. It was truly huge! The Fliffs had never actually *seen* Thunder and they only had a rough idea of his size. If his house was any clue, the Wolfhound was going to be pretty big. But then, when they heard Thunder snore, they KNEW! His snores sounded like boulders falling down a deep well.

Sherman's *fourth* doubt arrived when they went up the apple tree by Thunder's house and carefully climbed w---a---y out on the limb over Thunder's front door. One slip, one wrong move, and if Mister Thunder wasn't ultra-friendly, the game was over. Sherman could picture himself and Pop slipping, not being able to hold onto the branch, and falling. The rest of what might happen, he didn't want to think about.

So, as Sherman watched the Safety Cage swing back and forth and finally come to a rest in front of Thunder's front door, Sherman was out of doubts.

Earlier, when he had mentioned his concerns... worries, really... to Pop, his father had said, "Look, Sherman, don't worry. I'll bet Thunder has had a nice day and he will actually be glad to see us. Trust me."

Sherman had just nodded. He could not imagine that a Wolfhound would be glad to see a stranger, at his front door, at night, inside a tin can.

Well, Sherman was more right than he could have imagined. The fact was, Thunder's day had been just plain awful. At this very minute

Thunder was having a bad dream about a Cat who scratched his nose and came back the next day and ate his biscuits. In fact, Thunder's entire day had been lousy. Visitors. With bratty kids. The kids wanted to ride on his back and examine his teeth and when he was napping they opened his eye to see if he was really asleep. Then they yelled in his ear and poured ketchup in his water bowl. Thunder could have put up with that sort of nonsense if the kids' parents had made any effort to correct the little darlings. But no, they thought it was 'cute' and they also told the Johnsons that their dog needed to lose some weight. You could lose some weight, too, Thunder had muttered to himself—two brats' worth.

Anyway, in the midst of the bad dream about Cats, Thunder's alert nose detected a strange scent. He sniffed again. 'Hmmm, a different type of Creature. Probably another Trouble Maker,' he figured. 'Maybe if I go back to sleep... '

"Thun... der," called a strange voice that seemed to come from different directions. "Hel... lo..."

Thunder opened an eye. Then shut it quickly. He sighed wearily. He was having a *double* bad dream. He was seeing things that couldn't possibly be there. He *thought* he saw a cylindrical object right there at his front door. First, Cats, then metal cylinders. What a crazy dream.

He looked again. No, it was not a dream. It was a metal cylinder and it was rotating and there was a window in it. A window? Squinting, Thunder could see what looked like a small eye peeking out the window. This was even crazier than a dream! The thing in the can was a Creature and it could speak. How unusual.

"Pardon my ignorance," Thunder said in a soft voice," but what are you?"

When the window more or less settled facing the door, the voice replied, "I am from the Guinea Pig clan," a small, tinny voice said. "Fliff is the name, Fred Fliff."

"Very intriguing, Mister Fliff. Please speak up a bit. Tell me, does your kind travel by rolling?"

A nervous laugh. "Not by choice, no. Please, call me Fred."

"My pleasure, Fred. I am familiar with the Turtle clan. Their shell is different from yours. I assume it is a shell and not your true identity. And, I must ask, does your kind usually travel in the sky?"

"Oh no," Fred assured the Dog. "No to both questions. This shell is for dropping down from big trees. In case I am not, um, welcome?"

Thunder laughed. It sounded to Fred like thunder.

"You are welcome indeed. Do come into my home. Wear the shell if you feel uncomfortable."

Fred felt a little better. "Thunder," he said, "my son is in the tree and probably worried. May I tell him I am with a new friend?"

"Of course," the giant Dog boomed. "Invite him in, by all means."

"Sher... man," Father called. "Slide down the line and come meet Mister Thunder. Sherman?"

There was no reply.

"I hear something outside, Fred. Here, I'll take a quick look." So saying, the Wolfhound stuck his head out the door and immediately pulled it back in. "Fred, I do believe I have seen your son. He looks nothing like you, by the way. He has arms and legs and no shell. It is also my impression that he is preparing an attack. Please, reassure him that we are friends."

"Certainly. But first I have an important favor to ask."

"Ask away. But hurry. I prefer not to be at- tacked again today."

There was no reason to beat around the bush. Fred thought that Thunder was a reasonable Creature. "Can you ask... or tell... Hunter the Cat to leave us alone?" Fred said. "We mean him no harm and we'd appreciate the same courtesy from him."

Thunder laughed again. Now he understood everything. The shell was a protective covering, since Mister Fred and his son hadn't known what to expect, when they came visiting in the middle of the night. And he understood about the Cat. He definitely would have a serious discussion with Mr. Hunter, and it wouldn't be the first warning.

Thunder was just about to help Fred invite his son inside when there was a loud call from the house.

"Din din, Thunder. Here's dinner, big dog. Time to go."

Thunder looked down at his unusual guest. "Fred, I must leave immediately. Tonight is my night to go on patrol with Mr. Johnson and if I don't get up to the house for my snack, he will come down here. I really don't think it's a good idea for Mr. Johnson to see a Talking Tin Can or a small Creature armed with a sword." Thunder chuckled. "This has been an enormous pleasure," he continued. "Really! We must meet again. If you have a very high-pitched whistle, you can call me any time. Do you know how to whistle? You put your teeth together and blow."

"You betcha," Fred said.

"Good. Give a **Three and Three** call. I'll hear you. Meantime I shall speak to our mutual 'friend,' have no fear."

With that, Thunder stood, stepped out of his house... being careful to avoid bumping into the young warrior... and stood up.

Both Fliffs were astonished. The Dog was e—nor—mous!

" 'til next time, chaps," he called over his shoulder, and with that the Wolfhound was gone. He was out of sight in three bounds.

Fred climbed out of his tin can shell and tried to catch a glimpse of their new friend. Too late. Then he looked to his left and there was his son, standing there, mouth open, totally amazed. The boy had never seen the likes of a Creature like that. Nearly as big as a horse!

"That, my boy, is our new friend," Father declared proudly.

Sherman whistled softly. "I'm sure grateful for that, Pop. Wouldn't want him mad at me. Think he'll talk to that Cat?"

Fred looked off toward the Johnson's house. He could see lights on up there. No doubt Thunder was having his dinner now. His friend Thunder. He turned to his son. "I sure hope so, Sherman. That was very brave of you, by the way."

"I was kind of scared," Sherman admitted.

His father smiled and gently patted his son on the head. "That makes two of us. Well, my boy, we have accomplished important business tonight. A lot." Father was very pleased. "Tomorrow night, or the next, I might have a little surprise for the family. Let's go home. And let's be careful out there, son."

"That's my middle name," Sherman said.

CHAPTER 18

THE ZEBRA ZOOMERS

Father and Sherman stopped to rest in a thick hedge halfway between the Johnson's house and the Williams'. It had been a long trek, and a cautious one, because they were still watching for Hunter or any other Predator of the night.

"This looks secure," Sherman said, as he stepped through a thick cluster of hedge stalks.

Father turned and looked back toward the Johnson's. He could see part of the roof and mostly open space. Inside the hedge where Sherman was waiting looked well protected. The gaps between the stalks were close, which would prevent a large Cat from charging in.

"It does," Father agreed. "Care for some beet tea? Cold, I'm afraid, but nice and red."

"Red is good, Pop. Cold is, too."

Fred liked his son's attitude. Having an agreeable companion made life a lot more pleasant.

After checking twice to be sure the area was safe, the two adventurers removed their knapsacks, sat down, and broke out the beet tea and two cups. They sipped gratefully, then by turn sighed and let themselves relax.

"Mister Thunder sure is big," Sherman said, after taking a second sip of the cold tea. "He seems nice, too. That's kind of funny, isn't it."

"Funny? Why is that?"

"Him being nice," Sherman said. "I mean, because he's so huge and strong, he doesn't *have* to be nice. Who's going to scold *him,* right?"

Father thought about that a minute. Then he said, "I get you, but I think Thunder is nice because that's his nature. I have seen a Dog named Misha, who is a Golden Retriever. She too is big and strong and she has a very kindly disposition. Maybe Hunter would be nice if..."

"I sincerely doubt it," Sherman declared, interrupting.

Father laughed. "I doubt it, also, to be honest. But who knows, maybe if Thunder has a serious talk with the Cat, maybe he'll relax."

"Or maybe he'll change if they fix him," Sherman said.

Father winced, then nodded. "If they fix his attitude, that would be nice," he said. "But in the meantime we must continue to be vigilant. Are you about ready to leave? I know they'll be all excited to hear about our having met Thunder."

Sherman was ready. He wanted to get home... and he was curious about something. As they were getting the knapsacks on, Sherman asked, "You've been working on a secret project, haven't you, Pop? I know you have. That's okay. But why all the secrecy?"

"Why? Let me think about your question." Father thought about it as he took the Sun Bomb out of his pocket and made sure the battery was tightly attached. It would be very embarrassing if he whipped the flash bulb unit out to scare the Cat, and the battery had fallen off. Father gently tugged the wire. Good, firmly attached. He stuck his head out of the brush to check the terrain. Nothing looked out of place. "All right, my boy, let's go."

They went out carefully and proceeded west, toward the Williams' house. Its fancy turret was plainly visible over the gentle hillocks. Once the two Fliffs had a nice pace going, and their ears and eyes were tuned in to the moon-lit snowscape, Father returned to his son's question.

"I had an idea from something I'd seen on TV. So I just had to try it, Sherman. I had to! You see, we Guinea Pigs have a... a *spirit*, yes, that's the word... a *spirit* of invention and adventure. This spirit drives us to do unusual things. What's happening now is, the spirit is driving us in an entirely new direction. Maybe we are heading for a new Jungle. I just don't know." Father gestured broadly. "And we don't know all the Rules yet. So, probably I'm concerned about getting too excited about the idea, then discovering that it was too risky. That's why I have kept it a secret."

"Is that why we can't take Moonseeker out? Because we don't know the Rules?" Sherman asked.

"Sure. Well, we also don't know if the machine... No, wait, let me say it this way. We don't know *how* Moonseeker will behave when it's way up in the air, in the cold night with a wind. Or maybe Moonseeker knows how to fly, but we do not. Does that make sense, Sherman?"

Sherman thought about it as he moved alongside his father so they could talk in Secret GP Whispers. "Yes, I suppose so," he finally said. "But I'm wondering how anyone (he was thinking about himself) would learn to fly Moonseeker without actually flying it."

"Good point," Father acknowledged. "Maybe the only way to learn how to fly is the way we started to test it, before Hunter almost attacked us. Maybe we have to learn by degrees. You know, jump off a low rock first, then a bigger rock, and so on."

"Jumping off rocks? In this weather? With all this snow? It would have to be a darn big rock to test Moonseeker."

Father shrugged. "Maybe we'll just have to wait until summer."

Sherman was about to argue, and say *Summer? When* all *the hunters will be outside? That sure doesn't sound very keen.* But he didn't say it. He had learned that sometimes it was better to drop a discussion about Do's and Don't's <u>before</u> a parent issued an order (like DON'T).

"Let's talk about it later," Father said. "Tomorrow, when we're all rested. To answer your question, son, yes I am working on a project and no, it is not quite as..." Father was going to say 'risky' but decided to pick a softer word... "as *frisky* as Moonseeker. It will probably seem kind of dull, compared to the Wing. What can I say, Sherman? It's an Idea. We do the best we can."

"Can we test your Idea, Pop?"

Father laughed (softly). He admired his son's persistence. "Always remember the Jungle Rule, Sherman: "It is best to test... uh..."

" 'Before you messed... up,' " Sherman filled in.

"Exactly. And after some rest."

"What about Thunder?"

"I'm not sure if he can help us, either. I mean, suppose he doesn't get the chance to see that Cat. Or suppose he forgets all about us."

Sherman giggled. "I don't see how he could, Pop. I don't think he gets to talk to a Talking Tin Can every night. You did look pretty funny."

Fred had to laugh, too. "I reckon so. Anyway, what I think we should do is just face up to the challenges of our new, white Jungle and get busy with our Ideas. Sound right to you?"

"Sure does, Pop. And don't worry about Charlie not being enthusiastic about new Ideas. He's cautious, that's all. But brave, too."

Father smiled. He was so proud of his family. "If we do try out my secret project, it won't be for a few days. Also, it would just be an easy test. You know, get out there quickly, do a short test, and scoot back inside. Sound interesting?"

Of course it did. So the two adventurers in the New Jungle made a careful journey the rest of the way across the small hay field and onto the Williams' back yard. They stopped in hollows and waited, peeking over the top of small snow drifts to check for other Creatures and double-checking to be sure they were headed in the right direction for home.

It was a good journey. The air was cold and totally quiet. The moon's soft light gently washed over the tops and tips of mounds and bushes. Everything looked as if it were made from a magical mixture of ice, silver, and a trace of gold. A fairy land, it was, or maybe even a piece of the moon down here on Earth. Still, it was a pleasure when the great, spired Victorian house began to loom, high in the sky. Up there was the balcony, and the tiny door, and the passageway to Chloe's room. Home.

The unveiling of Father's secret project had to wait until a Sunday when the People were out and away, visiting recidivistic relatives at the pokey. When all was quiet in the house, Father simply slipped quietly over the side of the cage without making any announcements. Mother knew where he was going and she laughed to herself about how *subtle* Fred was. Mister Secret Project.

Fred made his presence known fifteen minutes later. **"Ahem,"** everyone in the cage heard from the floor. A rather loud 'Ahem,' followed by a second *Ahem*, then silence.

Mother winked at the children. "I think someone is calling us. Why don't we climb up to the top and take a look."

Before anyone got to the top, Mother said, "Close your eyes and no peeking 'til I say so. Don't fall, that's all."

No one fell and everyone obeyed. When they were all lined up, Mother called out, "OK, PEEK!"

Oh... my!

Down there on Chloe's braided rug were, not one, but **TWO** of the most spectacular pieces of racing machinery the Fliffs had ever seen! Side by side were **TWO** Zebra-striped bobsleds. They had sleek, rounded noses, windshields, enough cockpit space for three Pigs, glinting steel runners, brakes, steering wheels, pusher bars, and an electric black and white zig-zag paint scheme.

And seated ever so proudly in the nearest racing bobsled was Pilot Number One himself. Father was wearing his black winter Outdoor suit, goggles, black gloves, a white helmet, and a flaming red scarf.

"MEET THE ZEBRA ZOOMERS!" Father yelled.

Mr. Subtle, indeed.

For the next thirty minutes the Fliff family swarmed like ants on a candy bar, over, under, and in the Zebra Zoomers. They sat in the bobsleds while the others pushed. They skidded and turned and even raced the Zebras until, finally, after roaring around Chloe's room a dozen times, they were exhausted. Then, when they stopped to catch a collective breath, Father explained how the steering and the brake worked and what toys he had taken apart to make the sleds. All in all, the sleds were very cleverly designed and constructed.

As Father was answering Charlie's question about the wild paint job, Mother cut in.

"Everyone," she said, pointing to the window, "look. See where the afternoon shadow is? It's very late. Our People family will be back soon and we have important business to attend to. Fred, let's hide the Zebras and get back to the cage for our discussion."

Father nodded. "Absolutely, dear. Come on... Sherm, you take Zebra One, Rhodie, the other... into the closet. I'll show you where."

Like practiced teams, in three minutes the Fliffs had hidden the bobsleds and scrambled up the Climbing Lines into the cage. Though a bit tired, they were still excited about the Zoomers. They snacked quickly in order to discuss that important business.

Mother began. She had a serious expression on her warm face.

"Your father and I have talked about this," she said in a soft but hard voice. "We talked about testing the sleds, about going outside. It is risky. As clever as we think we are, we simply do not know what to expect. Those sleds are new and have never been tested. Are they safe? As much as I admire Father's work, we have to ask if the... um..."

"Zebra Zoomers," Oyster filled in.

Mother smiled. "The Zebra Zoomers are safe to ride in."

The children did not like the sound of this. They glanced at each other and shrugged their small but strong shoulders, as if to say: Does this mean No Sledding?

"I know the new Elevator can haul us up quickly," Mother went on, "and the Retriever might work well. But still, when we get out there in the open, we are vulnerable." She said *vulnerable* very deliberately. *Vulnerable* raised an image of a fanged Cat and helpless Pigs, of a stormy sea and Pigs on a coconut boat.

The young Fliffs began to slump in despair. No sledding...

"But that icy crust isn't going to last much longer," Mother continued. "And we... well, we are explorers, aren't we?"

The downcast eyes perked up. "Yes!" they all said in unison.

"Of course we are," Mother agreed. "Getting around is what we Pigs do. Why don't you carry on, Fred."

Grinning broadly, Father Fliff stood in front of his family. "I heard about a snow storm coming this way, tomorrow or the next day," he said.

"Fresh snow would make it impossible for sledding. Right now, however, the crust is solid. So, if we're going to test the Zebras, we should do it tonight. If you kids are tired, of course we can wait a week or two until..."

"WE ARE NOT TIRED!" sang out four young voices as one. Even Charlie had chimed in.

"If you insist, then," Father said, chuckling. "Straighten up, gang, here are the Rules. The Zebra teams: Mother will drive one Zebra, I'll do the other one. What we will do is one short test, to be sure everything works and nothing breaks. I can't tell you how important it is to test these machines carefully.

"Now, I don't think we'll have time to get them back up to the balcony, so we will have to dig a snow cave and hide the Zebras. Before we go out, however, we will be prepared to defend ourselves. Four Sun Bombs, swords, and a couple of silent whistles I found. Maybe they'd work against Cats, I don't know.

"Last but not least, everyone eat hearty and get some sleep... because... Ready?... because **WE GO TONIGHT!"**

Mother had to shush the kids, they were so excited and noisy. When they quieted down, she took care to remind them, "This will only be a short test tonight, so no complaining. I'm looking forward to that short ride; I hope you are, too." Mother made a Shhhh gesture.

"A test run," Father said. "Just a short trial run."

Everyone nodded enthusiastically. "Short," someone said. "Test."

The new and improved Elevator worked like a charm. One Zebra, then the other, was lowered down from the balcony without any embarrassing taps on the window. As soon as both sleds and the extra equipment were on the ground, the Teams lowered themselves to the ground. In very short order, six excited Fliffs were on the back yard, ready to try the Zebras on a gentle slope. They were wearing thumbtack spikes on their boots, so they wouldn't slip on the snow. Sherman took out one of the silent whistles and blew through it several times, curious how the darned thing worked. Not very well. He could barely hear it.

After Mother and Father checked the surroundings, they were ready. "Zebra Test Time," Father whispered. "Let's go. And remember, slow and low. This is just a test. Oh, one more thing..."

The children couldn't help it. They all groaned at the same time. One *more* thing? CAN'T WE JUST DO THE TEST?

Father knew how impatient they all were. He grinned, which was very annoying. Then he said, "There's been a change..."

Oh oh... oh no... COME ON, POP!

"...in assignments. Here is the new plan."

It was all the children could do not to shriek.

"A change in driver assignment. Hop in, kids. Mother and I will do the pushing to get us started. I hope we can have a safe, short test ride."

The four young Fliffs immediately elected Sherman to pilot one Zoomer, and Rhoda the other. In they went. When the two pilots were ready, they signaled the pushers. Mother and Father gave gentle pushes and the Zebras slid very nicely on the crusty snow. Of course they did. Maybe a little farther? Oh why not. The sleds went so easily, the pushers decided to hop in and go for a short ride. Just to the end of the lawn, then stop and hide the Zoomers in the snow cave.

That was the plan. A short test. Sure.

CHAPTER 19

WELL, WELL

The Zebras slid easily, all right. Too easily. Those smooth steel runners skimmed across the ice crystals like a meteor crossing the night sky. The two sleds picked up speed so fast, all the two teams could do was hold on, try not to smash into a tree, and try extra hard not to scream. Within seconds it was clear that the Zebras were going too fast to be stopped by the brakes. Within those first frightening seconds it was very **ultra-**clear that the *idea* of a short, slow, safe, and simple test was toast.

The two Zebra-striped bobsleds were *hurtling* down the biggest, steepest hill in town... in the **world**. Except for being gently steered, the Zoomers were out of control. The Fliffs, all of them, were scared stiff. Would they smash into a *million* pieces? If they didn't smash, where would they end up? A *m..i..l..l..i..o..n* miles away? How would they get home? Would it take a *million* years to get all the way back home?

But oh, goodness, those were just little problems, compared to the next part. Skidding, tipping, careening, bouncing, flying, they managed to survive Big Hill. They were chased by a gigantic Dragon, but they managed to escape by cleverly dodging in and out of the brush and rocks and trees, and everything... but they had escaped! They were so relieved.

But no, that was when the worst possible luck fell on them like a lead blanket. It was as if Mother Nature herself had decided to punish the

Fliffs. They had NOT escaped. The Dragon was waiting for them.

Yes, there it was, huge and menacing, like a Hawk, a Buzzard, sitting in the dark, waiting for them. The Beast, for that is what it was, was toying with them, scaring them, waiting, grinning, swishing its huge tail, baring its sword-sized fangs...

The Fliffs shut their eyes. They were doomed.

"WELL, WELL," spoke the giant Dragon. "TWO HOLES IN THE GROUND. WE MEET AGAIN."

The Dragon spoke. Its voice was like thunder and lightning.

A million thoughts flashed through Father's head. He pictured the warm cage back inside the nice big warm house. He pictured his children doing their homework by the water dish, sweet Betsy teaching them how to dance. Pictures from his entire life sped by. (It didn't take long.)

Father Fliff was terrified and also sad. How he would miss his family. He didn't think any of them had much of a chance of getting away from the Dragon. But, you can't give up. He pictured what he could do. Not much, but it would be something. If he boldly *attacked* the Creature, maybe his family could escape into the brush.

That was what he decided to do. Attack, and hope his family escaped.

In that very last instant before attacking the mighty Dragon, as he pulled a shuddering breath into his small but healthy lungs, Father just could not figure it out. He was absolutely puzzled. He wondered:

How... On... Earth... Had... All... Of...
THIS... **Happened**?

The only thought that came into his frightened head was something about— (Oh gee, it sure sounded silly now)—something about:

Getting around and Going Up Some Wall.

Oh well, Goodbye my loved ones. "**FLIFF ATTA...**" he started to yell.

"**Wait, Pop!**" his son screamed, "**Wait!**"

Father froze. Then, to his *horror,* he saw Sherman *leap* from the Zebra and *dash* toward the gigantic DRAGON.

OH NO... The End. Father knew he had to attack. He had to!

But wait... Wha-a-a-t?

Father couldn't believe his eyes. He ripped his goggles off, to be sure he was seeing this clearly. Oh Great Pigs of the Jungle, there was his son, Sherman Fliff, bravely *flinging* himself *at the feet of the DRAGON.*

Then Father watched with double horror as the DRAGON lifted a gigantic, clawed arm into the air and there was Sherman... SITTING ON THE CLAW AND WAVING AT THEM.

Father actually passed out for a couple of seconds.

Father awakened to a very strange sound. It was a rolling, deep sound, like thunder from distant mountains. But it was an oddly gentle sound and it did not cause him fear. Father listened, because he thought the sound was actually talking to him! How could that be?

"How nice to see you again, Mister Tin Can Fliff," the deep but kindly voice said softly. "And to meet your very excellent family. Have you recovered, Fred Fliff, and do you remember me?"

Father sat up.

"Of course I do, Mister Thunder," he managed to say. "I was hoping we would meet again."

A grateful tear rolled down Father's tautly rounded cheek. Oyster was sitting on Thunder's head, holding on with one paw and waving with the other. So *that's* how it happened, Father thought, feeling so thankful he didn't dare say it. It had all started with Getting Around. Who could have foreseen this?

For the next hour the Fliffs and Thunder talked and told stories and laughed and joked and had the very best time possible. The Fliffs were astonished at the Wolfhound's gentle ways and his polite way of speaking. They heard about the history of his kind, from a land far away, and they were amazed that a Creature so big and FAST could not only lead a life way different from theirs, but also that he was keenly interested in their stories.

The seconds flew into minutes and the minutes grew to hours. Finally, as the moon dipped and touched the horizon, they all realized there was much more to talk about, and so little time. Betsy Fliff interrupted the story-telling and explained to Thunder that if the Williams discovered them to be missing, they would be very, very worried. They might have a Search Party, whatever that was.

"Of course they would be worried," Thunder said. "I know the Williams. They are good people. Perhaps I can assist you in making a speedy return to the house?"

Thunder's offer sounded fantastic. The Fliffs said Yes, immediately. Before departing, however, they had to do two things: One was to find a safe hiding place for the Zebras. Thunder said he could take care of that very easily. The second item was promising to meet again, soon. All seven Creatures agreed.

So the Fliffs climbed aboard the giant Wolfhound, held on tightly, and away they went. It was a magic ride, up that hill, which now seemed so small as it flew by under the Dog's huge strides. At the edge of the Williams' back yard, the Fliff children kissed Thunder goodnight. A huge tear, a tear of happiness, rolled down his tawny cheek and over a tooth the size of a... a dragon fang.

In that parting was the start of a friendship the size of the world and the shape of a warm and trusting heart. Big Creatures and small, joined by trust, adventure, and the deep pleasure of companionship.

Getting around.

CHAPTER 20

Rhoda Fliff, AERONAUTICAL DESIGNER

"Do you think it'll work, Sherm? I mean r-r-*really* work?"

Rhoda's whisper shivered, as if she was nervous. Or cold. Or both.

"Well," Sherman replied slowly, "I guess so. I mean if you do exactly..."

"What'd you mean, '*I guess so*'?" she snapped. "This is no time for g-g-guessing, Sherman."

"What else is there!" Sherman snapped back. "This wasn't my idea, Rhodie, and the only reason I agreed to help was so you wouldn't break your foolish neck doing it alone."

Rhoda shivered again and took a deep breath. She knew her brother wasn't happy about this scheme, and she wasn't, either.

"I sort of w-wish Mom and Pop were here," she said wistfully. "Maybe I should've..."

Frustrated, Sherman whacked his smooth tan and white forehead. "Hovering hangnails, Sis! Look, we've been over this a beetillion times. Yeah, I wish they were here, too. But they aren't. So you decide: Go or Don't go. And hurry up, 'cause it's cold standing around and arguing."

Rhoda peered down into the darkness and saw how far away the ground was. Everything was cold, dark, and far away... including her enthusiasm.

Two days ago it had seemed so simple. She had grabbed her big brother and told him to meet her in the Workshop. Which he did.

Alone together, Rhoda had explained her idea to Sherman. She didn't want to worry Mom and Dad, she had said, so, would he help?

Sherman hadn't liked the sound of this plan, but he had gone along with it; he was curious, too.

But now, alone on a dark night and feeling deceitful, the two Fliff children were cold and unhappy. Finally, Rhoda said, through keen white teeth that were beginning to chatter, "S-S-Sherman, I'm never going to lie again. But I guess we'd better f-f-finish up what we started. Is the Retriever ready?"

"Yup,'" Sherman said.

"All s-s-s-set?" Rhoda asked, in a weak voice.

Before Sherman could answer, both children were startled by a soft voice behind them. Right behind them on the cold, dark balcony. The words chilled them more than the freezing air and breeze.

"We're sorry you felt the need to lie to us, dears," said the voice.

The words echoed in Rhoda's head and in Sherman's: 'We're sorry you felt the need to lie to us, dears.'

"M-m-mom... Pop... I... we... didn't hear... y-you."

Sherman tried to speak; his mouth opened and closed, but all he could utter was, "W... uh, w... uh, w... uh." That didn't sound very intelligent, so he shut up and waited for Doom to hit him and Rhoda.

"You k-knew what we... we were doing?" she stammered.

"Not exactly 'What' you were doing," Father said as he helped Mother climb up the railing. "Just that you two were up to something."

Sherman had recovered his voice. "How come y-you didn't just tell us to explain, like you usually do," he asked.

"How come?" Father said. "Mother and I were curious about the secrecy, but we decided not to meddle in your activities unless you asked us for help."

Those kind words struck both children in the softest part of their smooth round bellies. Tears welled in downfallen eyes. They felt ashamed. After taking a long time to gulp and swallow, Sherman struggled to say what his deepest fear was.

"You gotta be *awful* mad at us for, you know, for doing this without permission. We really... we really... let you... down." He could barely finish the sentence, he was so choked up.

"Mom, Pop, listen," Rhoda said urgently. "This is *my* fault. Sherm was only trying to protect me. Please, don't blame him. I deserve all the blame."

She began to unstrap herself. Rhoda sighed wearily. She was so ashamed of herself. In one silly moment she had managed to ruin her chance to fulfill her dream. And she had harmed Sherman, too. And how was she going to face the little kids? They'd know that their Big Sister had lied to Mom and Pop. Rhoda felt totally miserable. This was awful. Rhoda wished she could shrink down to the size on an Ant. (Why an Ant? Ask the ashamed one.)

Mother exchanged a signal with Father, and went over to Rhoda. "You're giving up?" she asked, in a soft, caring voice.

"Sure, Mom. No, I mean not 'giving up'. It's only... well, I mean I was wrong and... Oh bugs! I don't know what I'm trying to say."

Sherman was totally confused now, also. "Rhodie's sorry," he said with utmost sincerity. "Me, too. We'll do whatever you want, Mom, Pop. I guess the first punishment is not doing what we wanted to do."

Chuckling, Father patted his son on the back. "Don't jump to conclusions... so to speak. Mother and I haven't said No. We're disappointed you didn't ask us, sure. But we have watched you two work." Father checked the cables on the Control bars. "We've seen what good work you do and how nicely you work with little brother and sister. Most of all, we admire your sense of adventure. Both of you. Anything else, Betsy?" Father asked.

"Independence," she said. "We admire independence, even if you went for it improperly."

"Exactly! All right then." Father clapped his gloves. "You've had your punishment. If you want to go through with this, um, rather bold step, we will trust your judgment. Can we help?"

Rhoda and Sherman began to sniffle.

"Now, now," Mother said, her voice full of bounce. She hugged Rhoda, then her son. Father did the same. "Are you ready, or do you want to wait?"

"It's kind of far down," Rhoda said, hesitantly.

"Yeah, but the snow's pretty soft," Sherman said. "And deep."

Rhoda glanced down. *W-a-a-y down.* She lifted her proud head and looked at the yard and the trees and the Hill and the dark blue sky. She realized that something big had happened.

Something *truly* big. She and Sherman had been given a vote of confidence by their parents. Now she had to prove herself. It was the *Moment of Truth.* Summoning all her courage and all her strength and all her hopes, Rhoda lifted the huge red Moonseeker high over her head, pumped it to be sure the fabric was loose....... and jumped.

Yes, Rhoda Fliff *jumped.* Off the balcony! She held tight to the Control bar and pulled Moonseeker's nose down. The wing answered her command. It dove toward the ground and began to go faster. The cold snowy lawn seemed to rush up at her as the Rogallo wing plummeted downwards.

Rhoda was scared, but she remembered her brother's instructions: 'Pull the nose down, Rhodie. You need speed to fly. *Down!*"

As the snow-covered ground got closer and closer, Rhoda overcame her instinct to slow down. She aimed the Zoomer at a spot fifty feet away and clenched her teeth.

Remarkably, the Rogallo wing began to come alive. First the fabric fluttered, then it rippled, then it pulled tight. Summoning all of her courage, Rhoda kept the nose tilted down and tried not to notice how close to the snow she was going.

Then she heard a distinct **POP** as the wing filled completely, and a second later everything went silent. Rhoda felt her stomach go W*hoop*s and the huge red sail commenced to lift. It was pulling her upwards!

Now came the *second* Moment of Truth. Resisting the urge to push the nose sharply up, Rhoda held it slightly down, just a little, and the red wing picked up speed. It did! The ground was flying beneath her boots. Faster and faster. Then, waiting as long as she dared, she lifted.

Rhoda was flying. Moonseeker was humming happily over her head. Its nose was slicing through the air, eager to take her anywhere!

"FLIFFS AWAY!" she sang out.

Rhoda's dream had come true. Flying! Her very own Moonseeker was flying. In that instant Rhoda was part of the air and the sky and the stars and the winds. It was her Destiny. If she wanted to, she could touch the Moon. She had never been so happy in her life.

CHAPTER 21

LIVING IN THE SKY

Rhoda was so excited about the idea of flying. It had been her dream, hadn't it? How often she had pictured herself soaring over the hills and valleys in an aircraft she had designed. She, Rhoda Fliff, *Aeronautical Designer!*

And that was it, of course, her calling in life. As she put Moonseeker through a few maneuvers, and it responded so well, Rhoda had a *gigantic* understanding about herself. The root and the heart of her interest really was *designing* a machine that would fly. Oh, sure, she wanted to actually fly the machine, but for Rhoda the real thrill would be proving that her *design* was correct.

Sherman, on the other paw, was a flying Nut. He watched Bert's favorite TV show, '*Flighty Ideas*', and he gobbled up every article he had a chance to read (of which there were many, because Bert got all his father's flying magazines). Sometimes, now that the Fliffs could get up to the cage wall, Sherman walked around the edge and made believe he was an airplane ready to take off.

So it had been Sherman who coached Rhoda about the theory and the procedure of soaring. He had explained about air speed, filling the sail for lift, banking, climbing and diving, and the danger of stalling. Now, up in the night sky, Rhoda remembered everything Sherman had told her.

Leveling off, up high and safe, Rhoda listened to Moonseeker. The sail fabric of the wing

was quiet now, with just a tiny rippling noise. It sounded just right, exactly as her brother had described. She had plenty of altitude, so Rhoda pulled the pointy nose down and began a gentle dive toward Big Hill.

Moonseeker went precisely where she aimed it. Rhoda experimented moving the Control bar carefully in each direction, and shifting her weight, to see how her machine responded. Testing, it was called, and Moonseeker got an A + for a test score. She was thrilled.

At the crest of the Hill, Rhoda held her breath. Sherman had said that the air might actually be flowing *up* the hill. Keep the speed up, he had said, and fly around until you feel the wing *lift*. Rhoda did just that. Eureka! She felt slightly warmer air on her cheek, and sure enough, Moonseeker began to move upwards. Quite nicely, she was gaining altitude and the snowy landscape was falling away. Forty feet, fifty... Moonseeker wanted to fly!

Higher and higher she went. In seconds, Rhoda could see a landscape spreading out like her very own map of the world. It was an awesome sight. She could see Big Hill in its entirety, the Pond, and beyond, the Forest. The Forest was larger than she had imagined, and it ran onwards toward the big hills where the train was. Far beyond was another pond. Rhoda wondered where the horizon was and what was past that one. Another horizon? And another?

Suddenly she felt a pang of fear. Suppose I get lost, she thought. What had Sherman told her? *'Keep the wing full, Rhodie, and fly in a big circle if you think you're lost. Pretty soon you'll spot something you recognize.'*

Her brother's reassuring voice echoed inside her head. She pushed the control bar and shifted her weight. Moonseeker slowed and turned, as if obeying but waiting for further instructions. Quickly, Rhoda pointed the nose down and picked up speed again. She turned. Trying these maneuvers a few more times, Rhoda circled and continued to gain confidence. When she turned back toward Big Hill, she saw her house. How small it looked. But it was her house and oh, how good it looked!

As she was trying to see if she could spot her family, Rhoda felt another soft brush of warmer air. Not much, but enough for her to realize that this had to be a thermal, an uplifting of air, just as Sherman had described. Try to fly inside it, he had advised, so Rhoda twisted a little and began cutting soft arcs in the rising warm air.

Rhoda was amazed to see how high above the ground she was. That could have been a wee bit scary, for a Creature whose ancestors had lived on the floor of the Jungle, but Rhoda thought about it and decided that perhaps her ancient family had also climbed trees.

Laughing about that idea—fearless Guinea Pigs at the *tops* of Jungle trees—the fearless pilot pointed Moonseeker's nose down again and picked up speed. She turned and raced along parallel to Big Hill.

When the Moon was at her back, Rhoda could see her shadow on the ground, racing noiselessly over bumps, crashing into bushes and emerging undamaged on the other side. Once, she saw a small Creature jump, startled, when the wing's shadow passed by. She called down, "Don't worry, we won't harm you."

Bolder now, Rhoda turned toward Thunder's home and past that, the Pine Stand. Swooping low, she heard the flutter of wings. An Owl? But wait... didn't Charlie say that Owls flew silently? That was kind of scary. Suppose an Owl rose into the air to challenge her. No thanks!

Rhoda sped away.

How quiet the world is, she thought. And how large. Rhoda banked the wing and looked up at the sky and the stars.

Back home, Mother, Father, and Sherman watched anxiously. Once in a while they saw a strange little shape soar past the face of the moon. They knew immediately who it was and they were so proud.

"Golly, it flies real well," Sherman said wistfully. He wanted so much to be up there. "I bet Rhodie's happy as a clam."

"Rapture of the heights," Father said. "It happens to all new pilots."

Sherman thought about that. What an interesting Idea. Maybe ancestral Pigs had been tree climbers and maybe that was why he wanted so much to fly. Maybe his family was a brand new kind of Pig. *Flier Guinea Pigs!* Wow, that'd be different.

Didn't he wish that he could be the flier.

CHAPTER 22

TAIL-FIRST

Maybe Guinea Pigs not only spent some of their ancient life leaping about in trees, maybe they also developed the art of mental telepathy. Just as Rhoda thought again about her family, as she was glancing over her shoulder at the tiny Victorian farm house so far away, she noticed a blink of light. And another, and several more. The light went on and off, on and off, then paused. Of course! It was Sherman, signaling with their Secret Code Blinker.

Rhoda leaned and pushed the nose down slightly so she could make a wide sweep that would let her look, without interruption, at the signal.

"A... O... K," the signal read. Then another: "A... O... K."

Though chilly, Rhoda couldn't help grinning. She leaned left and right, causing the giant wing to roll back and forth lazily in the night sky. Another signal was coming...

"H... A... V... E" pause "F... U... N."

It was then that Rhoda remembered again how much Sherman wanted to fly and yet how generous he'd been when he said that she should try Moonseeker first. Well, when she landed, it was going to be his turn!

Rhoda also realized suddenly how cold she was. The insulated suits were great, but the cold air infiltrated every little gap between gloves and wrists, boots and ankles, and under her proud chin. Brrr... rr... r... r

"O... K... K... AY," she shouted to the stars and her friends and her family, "he... here w... we g... go!" Rhoda leaned right, pulled the nose down, and began to roar home. In an instant Moonseeker was going so fast it hummed. Rhoda congratulated herself for designing a Rogallo wing that really steamed.

Then it occurred to her that she was going to have to land Moonseeker. Oh oh...

Rhoda pulled up, to slow down a little and to try to figure out the right approach for a landing. This wasn't going to be easy. In fact, it was going to be tricky. There was the big Black Willow tree in the yard, and all those shrubs, and the fence. She felt a little panicky. Where would it be clear enough to land?

As Rhoda shivered, she looked over her shoulder at the broad, open area at the top of Big Hill. Lots of room there. But what a long walk to the house. At night. All by herself. What advice had Sherm given her?

"Don't slow down too much when you land," he had said.

"Why?" she had asked.

"Because," he said, "if you go too slowly, the sail will deflate and you'll simply drop."

"Oh, great. What happens if I land too fast?"

Sherman had shrugged. "Two possibilities," he answered: "One is, you land fast and touch down and you can't run fast enough. You trip, the wing flops, and you get buried in the snow." He had laughed at that.

"The other way is, when you're landing hot, at the last second you push the nose w..a..a... y up and you do a flare like most birds do when they land. You slow down fast and land. It's really neat."

'Oh yeah, neat,' Rhoda muttered to herself now, as she got closer and lower. Suddenly the house was looking bigger. Rhoda was just about to turn right and go around for another try when she remembered the last thing Sherman had told her about landing. *'You better get it right on your first try.'*

Being curious, Rhoda had asked *Why?*

'Because,' her brother said, *'because you don't get a second chance.'*

With that cheerful warning in mind, Rhoda decided to do the best she could and that was that.

Her angle of drop looked pretty good. Rhoda glanced up at the sail fabric—nice and full. She pulled the nose down a little, banked, and aimed at an area closer to the Willow tree than to the house. The wing fluttered, but filled again when she dipped the nose to gain speed. Lower... lower... Oh wow, was the snow coming up fast! Rhoda resisted the urge to slow down. Lower... lower... Wow—ie, this is fast!

At the very last second, when she could almost feel her cold feet touch the snow, Rhoda realized that she had, as Brother would've said, **'Over-cooked it.'** *Way* too fast. The idea of burying herself headfirst in a snow drift seemed horrible. But Rhoda knew what to do. Using all her strength, the brand new pilot pushed the wing's nose up as high as she could. What Sherm called a *flare*.

Moonseeker responded! For a moment it looked as if it was gathering power for a launch to the stars. The nose rotated up, the fabric filled, the wing practically jammed to a stop, and...

145

there... she.... was... looking at the sky... and Moonseeker simply dropped, backwards, tail-first, into the snow.

Embarrassed, Rhoda wanted to leap off the seat, jump down, and yank her machine out of the snow. She started to unbuckle the safety harness... and couldn't. Her fingers were stiff with cold. She tried to roll off her perch and that didn't work, either. Oh, she thought, isn't this fabulous. Either I freeze here and they'll dig me out in the spring, or Hunter will wander by and I won't have to worry about freezing.

She was trapped in her beautiful flying wing and there was nothing she could do about it. Trapped, maybe forever. How very sad. Rhoda hoped her family would remember how well Moonseeker had flown. Maybe they'd remember her, too.

A small, damp, chilled sob escaped the pilot's trembling lip. Just one. Then she said, out loud, "Darn it! This isn't right! Moonseeker can fly on moon dust and wind and here I am in a snow bank, STUCK! Not fair!"

CHAPTER 23

RESCUE

Father looked at his son. "Please explain yourself before I get very angry, Sherman," he said sharply. "And make it quick! Rhoda needs help **right now!**"

Sherman gulped. He knew his father was mad. He took a deep breath and stood as straight as he could.

"I *know* she does, Pop," he said, hoping his voice wouldn't shake. "That's why *I'm* going. I am. It's *my* fault the way Rhoda landed and it's *my* duty to rescue my sister. Besides..." Sherman had an idea how he might win this argument. "...besides, you're the one who's gotta haul her up, 'cause you're stronger'n I am. Please, Pop."

Then Father stood straight up, too, toe to toe with his son. Gosh, he thought, Sherman is taller than I am. How did *this* happen? He was about to say 'No, and that is final,' when he felt a firm hand on his arm. He knew who it was and what it meant. Father sighed and nodded.

"Yes, my boy," he said, sighing again, "I guess I can haul a line pretty well. You go ahead. I know you will do it right."

That was how they decided who would go after Rhoda. The rest was easy. Sort of.

Sherman attached the Retriever to the railing. He made sure the spring was wound up all the way. Then he attached one end of his rescue line to the Retriever and tossed the rest of the line over the railing. His father knew how to release the brake slowly, so the retrieve, or tow, line would come back to the balcony slowly.

147

His own shorter climbing line was hooked to the railing, too, and Sherman was ready. He slung the new show shoes over his back, saluted his family, and over the edge he went.

The snow had a good crust on it, so Sherman didn't need the snow shoes. He made quick progress to Moonseeker. Rhoda was fine, but her teeth were chattering. Sherm was able to pull the wing down a little and unhook his sister. She tumbled out of the small seat onto the snow. Quick as a wink, Sherman attached the Retriever line to his sister and explained how it was going to work. Rhoda tried to tell him about Moonseeker, who great it was, but Sherman wanted to get her home and warm, so he simply said "Sure" and gave his father the Three-Pulls signal to begin towing Rhoda home.

Retriever worked like magic. Rhoda skidded across the snow on her back. That was a funny sight, actually. It reminded Sherman of a movie he had seen about skiing on water, when the person falls but forgets to let go of the tow line.

When Rhoda reached the house, Sherman was pleased to see that Pop actually used the machine to haul Rhoda all the way up. As he watched his sister rise in slow stops and starts, Sherman felt better. Sis was almost safely back at home and she'd be in warm shavings and she would have all kinds of stories to tell. The little kids would be so excited. Sherman sure wished he could be telling the kids about flying, too. He patted Moonseeker. "This is the end of flying." Sherman sniffled. "It's not your fault—you did super good, Moonie. Really good job."

Oh, how disappointed he was.

Well, there was still work to do. Sherman got busy on the wing, wrestling it out of the snow, then dragging it into the bushes. It was quite an effort to conceal the magnificent machine, but he made quick work of the job. Before leaving, Sherman snapped a respectful salute to the now-hidden hang glider. "Goodbye, dear Moonseeker," he whispered. "Thanks for taking care of Rhodie."

Then Sherman turned towards the house. He was glad for Rhodie. She designed Moonseeker and she got to fly it. She deserved that, she really did.

But deep inside, Sherman knew he would never get to fly Moonseeker. When Rhoda jumped off the balcony, she nearly didn't make it. The balcony was not high enough for a safe launch every time. For a safe take-off, a pilot should have plenty of room and enough airspeed to completely fill the wing.

Landing was tricky business, too. Especially at night, when you couldn't see every branch sticking out. Landing on the back lawn was not a good idea.

Thinking about that sleek shape as it swooped across the sky, Sherman could just imagine how totally glorious it must have been up there. And he had to admit, Rhoda had been a braver pilot than he thought she would be. She went far away from the house. High, too. At the end, coming home, she really cooked when she flew back toward the house.

Sherman could just about hear the air rushing by and the wing fabric rippling at high speed. And he could hear how Mom had gasped when Rhodie had flown clear out of sight one time. Mom had been so afraid and Pop had to comfort her and say *It will be all right, Mother.*

No, Sherman doubted that his folks would go through that again.

Then there was the thing with Pop. That worried Sherman. He had actually *defied* his father. If Pop had said No, of course he would have obeyed. But maybe Pop had felt sorry for him, and that was the reason he had said to go ahead with the rescue. Yeah, that was it. Pop didn't want to embarrass him. Now, however, when he got home, Sherman just knew he'd be taken aside and they would have a *private conversation* about it and he would feel awful and the little kids would see it all, and...

Sherman sniffed and wiped a little tear away. Then he started across the lawn. Walk tall, he told himself. At least one Pig had flown. And Retriever worked right. Pig Pride! At least he could be proud of his Retriever and all the help he gave to Rhodie when they were building Moonseeker. Sometimes you gotta be happy just sharing success.

CHAPTER 24

(Sometimes just being
a good brother is rewarding.)

Days later, Sherman was on the edge, so to speak. Before a big step. He paused to let his thoughts settle down. A little thought came to him. Take the *dis-* away from *dis*appointment and you have a new word: 'Appointment.' Maybe I have an *appointment*. With what, he wondered. With fate? No, he thought. Fate sounds kind of nasty. What's a better Idea? Then it came to him: An appointment with **Destiny**! Keen. If he ever built an airplane, he would call it *Destiny*.

But Sherman had other things to think about. Like not making a fool of himself. Sherman Fliff felt his heart beating fast again. He knew what it was. He was... the word *scared* came to mind, but Sherman rejected that. He wasn't scared; he was *ap-pre-hensive*. That was it, apprehensive. And who wouldn't be anxious, or apprehensive? If this didn't work, he sure was going to feel silly. To say nothing of feeling sore, if he crashed. With everyone watching. Oh well, now or never. Sherman looked to his left and nodded.

"All set," his helper whispered. "Do it, big brother. **GO** !"

Sherman went.

Did he ever. Sherman was holding Moon-seeker overhead and standing, balancing, on a thing that looked like a snowboard. The board had a track on its underside, and the track ran on the strong line that stretched from the balcony all the way out to the Willow tree. His invention was called Wing Launcher, and the idea... the hope... was that the long, downward slide on the line would get him going fast enough to fill the wing.

The Launcher worked. With Sherman and Moonseeker balancing on it, the launcher plummeted down the line like a runaway rocket. Moonseeker went so fast its wings popped when the fabric filled and before Sherman even had a chance to think, the hang glider lifted him off the Launcher and he was airborne. **Airborne!** Sherman pulled the nose down a little and banked into a turn. He had good airspeed when he flew past the tree trunk, over the bushes, and out. Sherman couldn't believe his eyes... suddenly he was beyond the big back yard and on his way into open territory and Big Hill. In the air! This was his life's dream come true.

Grinning, the pilot wiggled more comfortably into the small seat and then wiggled the Control bar, to be sure Moonseeker was behaving properly. It sure was! The flying machine seemed to wiggle back, as if to say, *'Nice to fly with you, Mister Pilot. What do you have in mind?'*

Sherman had to laugh out loud. Have in mind? How about some velocity! At the crest of Big Hill, instead of beginning a gentle climb to gain altitude, Sherman plunged downslope. He hugged the hill until Moonseeker's control lines began to thrum.

The ground rushed by and though Sherman paid constant attention to the flight path ahead, he nonetheless caught glimpses of bushes and bumps, of shadows and shapes.

Then, wisely aware that a pilot must not let his attention get fixed on the ground, Sherman lifted his proud chin and the wing's pointed nose at the same time. Ahead was the Pond and to the right was the area where Rhoda said she had caught the thermal uplift. Moonseeker leveled off nicely and as if sensing what Sherman wanted to do, began circling.

But he wasn't ready for easy going yet. After he had climbed—and the wing lifted grandly—Sherman headed down again and banked Moonseeker in quarter-rolls, back and forth, back and forth, to get a sense of how she reacted. He had a good ear for the sail and could tell when the wing needed more speed, more air. No prob. Level off, dip, fill. What a great design! Sherman was so proud of the job his sister had done.

Altitude. Sherman found the edge of the thermal updraft and experimented climbing. Keeping an eye on the night sky and where home was, he kept going up. By banking slightly, Sherman was able to see upwards. It was a Socko sight. All the way up to the stars! But it was birds he had in mind when he turned, not the stars. One special bird! When he had enough altitude, Sherman pulled the nose down and plummeted out of the sky like a bird he had seen on TV. A Falcon.

Back home, Rhoda had seen all of it, even when Sherm was only a speeding arrow in the sky. "Wow, wow, WOW," she shouted, jumping up and down. "It's incredible! It's as if Sherman has been flying all his life."

Father chuckled. He stood on tip-toe. "Almost," he said.

"I hope this isn't his last flight," Mother said. "He is putting an awful lot of strain on those wings."

"If he goes any faster," Father remarked, as he caught sight of the new Falcon in the sky, "the speed will shred his nice warm flight suit and he'll arrive home in just his shorts and boots."

Everyone laughed nervously. But really, there was nothing to do except trust Sherman to use his head.

Which is exactly what the lad was doing. He pushed the nose up a little, cut into a wide turn toward the Wild Wood, and began to climb again. Sherman wanted to see the sky now, and he just wanted to absorb the majestic feeling of flight and freedom and space.

The air was cold, up high, but the sky was so clear Sherman imagined that he and Moonseeker were the only link between Earth and Space. The distance was not so far—there, up there, were the stars and galaxies and other moons and suns and Moonseeker seemed ready to reach as far as its pilot wanted to go. Maybe he could ride the thermal for miles and miles.

Way far away, where the horizon blended with the sky, Sherman saw the setting moon. Hey, Mister Moon, it's me, Sherman Fliff. How large and beautiful, that mottled silvery disk. He imagined that the odd markings were words meant for pilots to read when they got close enough: *Try to touch the moon.* Funny, that's what Rhoda had said, when they were building the Launch Skate Board. Maybe she had seen the words, too.

Those words lingered in Sherman's head. He thought he saw the Man in the Moon wink. Sherman grinned. "Someday, Mr. Moon," he shouted. He couldn't wave, because a smart pilot keeps both paws on the controls at all times.

The words 'Smart pilot' and 'Test Pilot' now came to Sherman's mind. They were reminders of an excellent article he had read. Test pilots are not wild and crazy fliers. No. They get the job done because they are smart and careful. Okay, bold, too, but they bring themselves and the aircraft home, safely, in one piece, for more flights. Glancing over his shoulder, Sherman nodded to Mr. Moon. "Say hello to Mister Mars for me, will you? Bye."

He banked and turned until he saw his home. It was small and so far away. Like a toy house, really, a toy house sitting on a mound of snow. Tiny Creatures, loving Creatures, were way, way down there watching him. And there, way to the left and East, was Thunder's toy house. (Sherman had a hard time imagining Thunder as being a toy.) 'Here I come,' the test pilot said to himself. He pulled the nose down and away he went.

Sherman knew something about Moon-seeker now. It was strong and if it wasn't happy with what the pilot was doing, the hang glider would warn him. So Sherman knew he could really fly it fast, and he did. Sherman flew so fast, the cold, roaring wind tore a package of carrot biscuits out of his pocket. He glanced down, but it was too late. Some critter was going to enjoy a surprise tomorrow morning.

Going home. It was a good feeling. Sherman Fliff was proud of himself. The adventure in the sky had changed the lad. The world was so big and the sky was even bigger. Part of him had come from the Jungle and part of him would always live in the Sky. In a way, he had touched the moon. Certainly the moon and the stars had reached out to him.

That's the secret, isn't it, Sherman said to himself. You start with an Idea. Then you learn about the Idea. Then you work as hard as you can to make the Idea work. Maybe it will, maybe it won't, but you keep trying. And then, finally, you reach a place on the ground, in the air, in space, *where you and it are connected*. Where you *want* to go, where you work hard so you *can* go, that is the final frontier, isn't it?

Yes, he said, answering his own rhetorical question, and the ultimate gift is when you share your Idea to entertain and inspire others.

CHAPTER 25

FLIFFS and PEOPLE

The next two weeks melted away like icicles in an oven. Rhoda and Sherman were still high with excitement about their adventures in the night sky, and of course the little kids were clamoring to be given their chance to soar, too.

Fred Fliff was eager to try the wing, and he kept encouraging Betsy to give it a try. He spoke about building a second Moonseeker, so they could fly together. And of course the smaller team members squawked about having smaller wings built for them. Five new wings would be nice, thank you.

And not only that excitement, but another world had opened for the Fliffs—their beginning friendship with Thunder, the huge Wolfhound.

All in all, the Fliff world, or the Fliff Jungle, was getting larger by the day.

Getting up and down from the cage was so easy now. The Fliffs were comfortable with exploring the large Victorian farmhouse. They explored very carefully, however, for two reasons. Well, actually one reason: they did not want to meet the Cat **or** the Williams. (But for different reasons.)

Then, in between talk about "banking the wing" and "reaching for the moon", the young ones had to stay on top of their studies—geometry, geography, geophysics, and geology this winter. As father said so often:

"A Pig's mind is as big as the next lesson And once more."

No one understood exactly what Pop meant, but so what. Lessons were fun, and the children now knew how lessons, if learned, were a ticket to the outdoors, to Zoomer sleds, and to the very skies.

What about the Zebra Zoomers? The Zebras were a measure of the winter weather. If it had just snowed, the sleds couldn't be used. If there was a crust on the snow but the day had warmed up too much, the sled runners cut through the crust and stopped dead in their track. Only when there was a hard glaze on the snow was it possible to slide on that surface and zoom down the Hill. They went out twice. The Zebras were very fast and Mother and Father had a feeling that Sherm and Rhoda were hoping for a big Race someday soon. First things first, however.

Chores and repairs were *first things*. The children were used to doing chores around the cage, but now they had extra duties—such as keeping the winter suits and the equipment clean and repaired. Oyster tore a hole in the seat of her cold suit when she fell out of a sled and slid down part of the hill sitting down. Ooops.

The snow cave where they hid the Zebras got soft and collapsed one weekend, so the entire family had to dig the sleds out, build a framework out of sticks and pack snow around it, sort of like a reinforced igloo. Thunder helped them on that project.

During the day and early evenings, the Fliffs were simply the cute, furry Fliffs when Chloe or Bert wanted to play. They read books and watched some TV. (The Williams children were only allowed to watch one hour of TV a week.) The Pigs spoke in their usual *Squeak Language* to amuse the Williams, but one time this deception nearly backfired. Here's how that happened:

The Fliffs understood Two-Leg talk, of course. Well, one evening Mrs. Williams had the job of feeding the Pigs and she absentmindedly asked them if they were hungry. Charles, who was tired and hungry, replied "YES I AM." And a very surprised Mrs. Williams said "My goodness, can you talk?" To which Charles said, "CERTAINLY." The other Fliffs, eyes and mouths popped open in horror, looked at Charles.

Luckily... very luckily, Charles was using *Squeak Language*. But Mother and Father both noticed that Mrs. Williams smiled when she put the fresh pellets next to their youngest son. Then she winked at Mother and Father. Hmmm. Maybe People Creatures were smarter than the Fliffs had thought.

What did Mother and Father decide to do about building a second flying wing for themselves? Or smaller ones for the smaller children? This was interesting. First, Mother declined the family's encouragement to fly. Next winter, she said. They pleaded with her, and reassured her that it was fun and not dangerous, but Mother said No thank you, not now.

A second Moonseeker, big enough for two? No way. They wouldn't be able to hide it. Okay, what about smaller ones? Sorry, not this year. Mother and Father told the little ones that they had to be at least a year older and as wise as their older siblings before they could fly.

"But you trusted them, Mom... Pop... it isn't fair!" (Oyster)

"Yes it is fair. Rhoda designed the wing and Sherman helped her and they are old enough and wise enough."

"But..."

"Your mother makes an excellent point. And she does have some seniority." (Father)

"And she's a LOT wiser," Charlie added, making a face at his sister.

So that was the end of that discussion.

One night when the North Wind had calmed and it was time for bed, Father looked up at the window and saw that the stars were bright and clear. "Later on," he whispered to Betsy, "Let's go out to the balcony and just *look* at things. It'll be fun... and quiet." He winked.

Mother knew what he meant. *Quiet* meant without the kids. She rolled her deep brown eyes and nodded.

So they did. When the children were sound asleep, Mother and Father went over the side of the cage, got their Winter Suits, and slipped through the secret passageway out onto the balcony. (They left a note with Sherman, who was the lightest sleeper, telling him where they were.)

It was very cold but also very quiet and beautiful. From their perch high up over the back yard and over everything that lay near and far, the Fliff parents had a grand view of their Snow Jungle. Very carefully, so as not to sneeze, Mother drew the clean, cold air into her healthy body. "Oh my," she said, "I remember standing on the pellet dish and trying to reach way up the cage wall. It seems like such a long time ago, Fred."

He laughed. "It was, dear. From the Green Jungle to the White Jungle by Magic Carpet is a long journey. It was easy, once we put our minds to it. This may be a new chapter in the *Grand History of the Guinea Pig*," he said proudly.

Mother was quiet. Then she said, "Very true, Fred. Everything has changed, hasn't it."

Now it was Father's turn to think. Finally he said, "Still changing, I think. We have some big decisions to make soon."

"Are you afraid?"

"Oh yes," he replied. "Not afraid as in *scared*, like I was when I was on top of the cage wall and scared *silly* about falling a million miles. This is a different feeling, my dear. The way we are now, we'll be going into the unknown and sooner or later our Two-Leg family will know."

Mother leaned forward and turned and looked at Fred. "I think they already do. They are smart Creatures, you know."

It was Father's turn to nod, then adding, "They do have potential. Perhaps in another few hundred thousand years they will evolve into Creatures like us. That would be fun, I think. There is so much we could show them."

"And in another few hundred thousand years we will be flying Moonseekers to Mars," Mother said, laughing.

Just then they saw a 'shooting star' that flamed bright, spiraled, and left a tiny plume of smoke. The Fliffs made a wish.

CHAPTER 26

WORRIES...

Mother Fliff awakened with a start. She had heard a strange noise, and in her sleepy mind it sounded like hailstones hitting the window. Blearily, she opened one eyelid and looked for the strange sound. It was Chloe, pouring pellets into an empty dish.

"Hi," Chloe chirped cheerfully. "Glad to see you're awake. The way you guys have been sleeping so late, a person would think you'd been up all night. Lay-zee, lay-zee," she scolded in fun. "See you this afternoon, Piggies," she called, and dashed off to school.

Chloe had no sooner made her departure, Mother shook Father. "Wake up!" she whispered sharply in his soft but esthetically proud brown ear.

Father flinched as the Mighty Beckons echoed painfully in his head. "Do I have a choice?" he grumbled.

"No. Did you hear what Chloe just said, about us being up all night? Do you think she peeked in the cage one time when we were out?"

Oh oh, Father thought. "Of course not," he said, hoping not to initiate a panic. "She would have called her parents, and they would've called *their* parents, and before you say 'Pigs Away', there would have been an *entire town* in here, Betsy."

But Mother had lingering doubts. "They know," she declared. "I know they do."

Father's eyes were still closed, and he was pleasantly warm in his bed of flannel and cedar

162

shavings. He wondered if he could get back to sleep. "Why don't we discuss this very thoroughly... uh-h-h-h-..." Father yawned mightily "...well, why not tonight?"

Mother shook her head. "Can't," she said. "We have a big meeting with Thunder, remember? Something mysterious you two have been cooking up. You know, Fred, you and Thunder..."

"And Charlie."

"Oh, yes, the Three Musketeers. Frankly, I'm concerned..."

"My name is Fred, not Frankly."

"You are not amusing, Fran... Fred! Pay attention, will you? I am concerned that we aren't being careful enough and we aren't considering the alternatives. There is so much... much..."

"Change," Father filled in. "C-h-a-n-g..."

"I know how to spell *change*, Fred," Mother said piquantly.

"Of course you do, dear. But you must remember this: It is easier to *make* change than it is to, uh, to change yesterday. Yes, that's right." He sat up. And yawned again. He glanced at the children. They were awake, but making believe they weren't. Listening.

"Betsy, dear, I understand your concern. I do. Why don't we mull this over for a day or two, then have a nice Family Council discussion."

"Yea!" a small voice said. It was Oyster. She loved Family Council because she was allowed to complain about Charlie, or declare that she was entitled to stay up later, and it was okay to say that.

When Mother heard Oyster's chirp, she had to grin, even though she was still worried. "All right," she said, sighing. "Time to get up. Tidy up, everyone. We have a lot of work to do today and a big mysterious adventure tonight. But don't forget, Fred, Family Council..."

"Tomorrow. Or next day for sure," Father said. "Charlie, I want you to make a list of what we'll need tonight. The sky was clear last night, which means it was cold. Therefore..."

"The crust will be hard and fast," Sherman put in.

Everyone cheered. Especially Charlie. The idea of flying definitely did not appeal to him. He might try it, if he had to, but not as a first choice. But sledding? A.O.K. Sledding was so much safer. Sure, the Zebras went fast and could crash, but you were always ON the ground. And you were always IN something! Charlie was pleased. He liked plans and the idea of mysterious adventures. (As long as they were on the ground, thank you.) What could go wrong if you were ON the ground? Nothing. Not. A. Thing.

CHAPTER 27

The BIG RACE

"Double rations tonight," Father said, as he tightened his boots.

Charlie and Oyster were way ahead of him. They had managed to eat triple helpings of dessert—tomato, apple, and wheat biscuits. The others had already packed extra food in their backpacks. Food and vegetable tea, plus an extra large portion, which Father carried.

When the town bell tolled 11:45 PM, the Fliffs rappelled over the cage wall to the floor in less than a minute. They moved through the bedroom darkness to the closet as silently as shadows.

At 11:49 PM they were on the snow behind the house, and three minutes later they were digging the Zebras out of the hiding place under the bush. Father had already signaled their new friend.

At exactly midnight on this cold February night, beneath a dark blue sky that reached across the wind to the stars, they were ready. The conditions were perfect. Goggles were on, helmets tight, runners cleaned and waxed, brakes and steering double-checked, windshields clean. This was the Mysterious Adventure! A RACE. This was for real.

Team One against *Team Two*. The rules were simple: (1) No bumping into each other, (2) To the Pond, (3) Be careful. That was it.

The two teams stood by their sleds, breathing deeply and flexing their strong Guinea Pig muscles... waiting.

Then, from a distance came the unmistakable call of their mighty friend. Thunder was on his way! Four Fliffs jumped into the sleds and tucked themselves in, and the two Pusher Fliffs began their work. The Race was on.

The first hundred feet on the icy crust was smooth sledding. There was the familiar mechanical noise of runners bumping over tiny ice hills and ridges. But then, as the Hill dipped and began to pull the Zebras faster, the bumpy clicking sounds turned to chatter. Very quickly, the chatter changed from Tac Tac Tac to TcTcTc, and finally to a steady Kkkkkk-k-k-k sound that sounded like a knife cutting thick paper. It was an insistent sound that came to your ear and said *'Pay attention, bub. Because we are trucking!'*

Then, as the Zebras began to dive down and down and faster and faster, the sound from the steel runners changed. It was like silk ripping. Oh, it was a glorious sound, one that very few Guinea Pigs had ever experienced. But the Fliff racer teams recognized it immediately. This z-z-z-ing sound meant speed, and plenty of it.

Ahead, wa-a-a-y ahead and down and far away, was a small dark area that sat amidst the raw white snow of the Far Fields. It was the Pond. The Moonseeker pilots had flown over the Pond, and they had seen that it meandered around to the west and seemed to link with a dark streak in the distance. Perhaps that was the River. The Fliffs didn't know. They had never gone as far as the Pond with the Zebras—too far.

Until tonight.

In order to reach the Pond, they knew they would need every ounce of speed the Zebras were capable of. The crews huddled low in their cockpits to cut wind resistance and to avoid the chilling wind that was becoming a hurricane as they went faster and faster.

The crews had to move carefully in the rocketing sleds. If someone nudged the steering wheel or leaned too far, the Zebra might skid, and if that happened, all control would be lost. There were too many rocks and bushes and small trees on the Hill—you had to be supremely careful.

Some might think that a Guinea Pig lacks the athletic skill to steer correctly on steep hills. That is completely not so. Pigs have superb coordination and balance. Also, because of their earliest days in the Jungle, GPs learned how to thread their way around vines and vipers, piranhas and pumas, while racing to a safe home. By instinct and experience, they are Creatures of speed, accuracy, and daring.

Other Creatures (including some who are very nice) might have slowed down, on the steep parts of Big Hill. Not the Fliff teams, no. They coaxed the Zebra sleds ever forward, thrilled by the short W-H-O-O-P-s flights as the sleds sailed off small mounds of frozen crust.

Once in a while a steel runner scraped across the top of bare rock, which caused a spray of golden sparks to light the underside of the sled. First, one Zebra took the lead, then the other. Back and forth they went.

At the mid-Hill open area, which was smooth and steep, the two sleds pulled alongside each other so the teams could wave. But then Pilot One pointed downhill and both teams refocused on the paths ahead. Very wise move!

The final part of the Hill was tough territory. There were large, snow-covered rocks here and there, trees and brush, and sections where you couldn't see what the trail looked like just ahead. There was no room for error here. None. You had to get it right the first time.

The two teams had just selected a route between two sharp hillocks when Father pointed up. He pointed with great vigor. Everyone except the Drivers glanced up. They saw an awesome sight! Silhouetted against the winter sky and flying off the hillock on the right came a Creature that seemed as large as a racehorse and as fast as the North Wind itself. Even in that split second when he sailed over their heads, the amazed onlookers could see his keen eye, his gleaming white teeth, and his warm smile.

"F-L-I-F-F-S," he called, his deep, friendly voice booming over the countryside.

"T-H-U-N-D-E-R," they all called back, six voices strong.

The race was truly on.

On the short parts of the Hill the Zebras actually sped ahead of the Wolfhound, but when they steered around an object Thunder bounded over it and took the lead. Back and forth this race went, over and around, gallop and a skid, an **O-h-h-h-h** and a WOOF.

On the final stretch of territory before the Hill leveled out, Thunder was ahead of the Fliff teams and was galloping around a large ten-foot high boulder, rather than leaping off it. As fast and strong as he was, Thunder did not relish the idea of such a tall jump. But the Fliffs had no choice. If they skidded around the rock they would slow a little and let the mighty Dog get

head. So, the choice was clear. Over and off the
top of the rock they went.

Suddenly the humming, ripping sound of
eight steel runners on icy crust stopped.

Everything went silent. Thunder looked over his shoulder to see what had happened. Imagine his surprise when he saw... above his head... the underside of one, then a second Zebra slider. He laughed. And held his breath as he waited for the speeding sleds to land.

By a miracle of Mother Nature both sleds landed hard but they did not break the crust. (If they had broken through the crust, the sleds would have stopped in their tracks but the teams would have continued on, tumbling, sliding, slipping, careening, catapulting, and somersaulting out of control. Not good.)

The sleds bounced and sped across the level section toward the Pond. As the Zebras slowed, Thunder caught up and ran alongside.

"Ready, Master Charles," he called over.

Charlie flung a long rope over to Thunder, who caught the end. Then it was Oyster's turn. When Thunder gave her the OK nod, she tossed her rope to the Dog.

Now, with both ropes in his white teeth, Thunder bounded ahead. Soon, all three were speeding toward the black ice. At the very last instant before he might leap upon the ice, Thunder released the ropes and turned sharply to his right to avoid getting hit by the Zebras, which sped ahead and onto the Pond. When the Zebras got on the ice, they seemed to rush forward like liquid lightning. They ran fast and silently, straight as arrows. One hundred feet, two hundred... two hundred and fifty... then they began to turn.

Slowly the turns twisted around, faster, faster, until both sleds were spinning crazily. Just as the whirling dervishes threatened to toss their riders off onto the ice, the Pushers yanked up on the brake levers. A fiercesomely loud *hissing* noise filled the winter air as two **majestic** showers of ice crystals were torn loose by the brakes. The ice sprayed into the night air like a fountain.

Thunder watched the spectacle from the shore. It was as if the Pond had sprung lunatic geysers. Looping plumes of sparkling particles coursed in magic arcs. It was a glorious sight. Thunder chuckled and shook his head. He had never had such fun before.

In less than a minute, however, Momentum's gift was spent. The Zebras slowed and stopped. The race was over. Thunder went carefully on the ice and pulled the sleds to the shore. Then he started up the Hill, with the sleds in tow.

A half-hour later they stopped in a protected cove that was guarded by a large boulder on one side and dense juniper bushes all around. Thunder had been here before, and had dug a nice hollow where they could not be seen and where they were out of the wind. It seemed warm in the hollow, when they could hear the fresh wind on the other side of the juniper bush and see the cold stars in the night sky.

Everyone was tired and excited. Oyster and Charlie climbed onto Thunder's strong neck while the other four built a small camp fire and unpacked the food. Charlie poured tea for everyone.

Oh my, didn't that warm apple tea taste good! The veggie bars did, too, including a nice big one for Thunder. They sat back with their feet toward the fire and ate slowly and sipped their drinks and kept saying over and over, *'What glorious fun that was!'*

That race had been adventure, for sure. The incredible speed, the huge thrills, the splendiferous spins on the ice, racing... everything. But the Grand Prize they shared equally was being together, family and friend, in the Great Outdoors.

CHAPTER 28

WINTER CAMPING

"What a dandy little stove," Thunder said. "Just the ticket for a chilly night like this. Did you purchase it at a very fine sporting goods store, Master Charles?"

"Oh no, sir," Charlie replied proudly, blushing beneath his tan and white fur. "I fig'ered out how to make one and Rhodie'n Pop got the parts from Bert's toys and we done... we *did* the work in the Secret Work Shop."

Thunder knew this, of course, but he wanted to compliment the young Fliff. No one corrected Charlie's grammar, either, because the family was so pleased Thunder had asked for a second cup of tea that had been heated over Charlie's stove.

"Well, then," the gentle Wolfhound said, "perhaps you can spare me another of those extraordinary biscuits your mother has made. I do have an appetite this evening."

Anyone would have an appetite on a night like this. Small pellets of frozen rain fell on the tarp that was suspended over their heads. It was a pleasant sound, a light tapping noise that made everyone very glad to be protected against the weather of the January thaw. Rain, sleet, and warming breezes from the southwest had softened the crust on the snow, so of course the Zebras were sidelined. And there wasn't a chance that anyone would fly in this weather, either. But the Fliffs and Thunder had gotten together for an Expedition they called 'Winter Camping'.

Mother put another batch of her tea mixture together—mashed barley cubes, orange slices, dried lettuce leaves, and apple slices and snow—in the heating pan, while Father unpacked Savory Grain Cakes, Celery Delight, and for their large friend, a big Carrot and Banana Biscuit. Everyone crowded around Charlie's stove while the tea heated. Small feet warmed quickly near the hot stove. In short order the goodies were ready for consumption, and they all did exactly that.

When Thunder was through, he licked his chops appreciatively and thanked the Fliffs for such a treat.

Mother smiled. She looked up at him. "You are most welcome. We thank you, too, Thunder. The children are too shy to say this, but I will. Our lives have been enriched by meeting you, *Mister Dragon*."

Everyone laughed, including the Wolfhound. Then his face got serious. "You have shown me a new life, Betsy and family. Although we are slightly different in size, I think of you as my brothers and sisters. Perhaps this is a good time for you to tell me about the idea Sherman and Master Charles have come up with."

The two lads practically leapt to their feet. Sherman unpacked the drawings while Charlie made a table from the plastic toboggan Thunder had used to haul the tarp and supplies. They spread the drawings out and Charlie explained his idea.

Thunder studied the sketches and listened carefully to how such-and-such was needed, where this-and-that should be placed, and how they could change a *whatchamacallit* to a thingamajig. The Wolfhound was especially impressed with how the Fliff lads had divided the work between small Creatures and a large one. He frowned, tilted his massive head this way and that, and nodded at some of the ingenious ideas the Fliffs had come up with.

The others watched and waited anxiously. They saw how comfortable the two lads were with the very large Dog, and saw also that Thunder seemed to have a good understanding of the plan. Mother and Father nudged each other when Thunder said such things as "Good thinking on that opening" and "What a novel idea!"

Finally, when they were through, Thunder looked around and said slowly, in his deep voice, "No, I don't think..."

The Fliffs gasped. Oh-h-h N-o-o-...

"...there will be any problem at all," he continued. "One minor detail to be worked out, but we can solve it easily." Thunder looked down at Mother and Father, who nodded at him. (That meant 'we will talk later'.)

Spirits soared.

"Yes," he continued, "construction looks possible. Naturally I defer to you Fliffs. You are the Engineers and I am the Helper. Whenever you decide to embark on this plan, count me in."

The Fliffs cheered, and to celebrate the Agreement, all seven Creatures shared the last sips of tea and crumbs of biscuit.

Spirits remained high as the campers returned their campsite to its original condition— fire out, utensils washed and packed, every bit of scrap picked up. When they were ready to leave, Father looked around and asked, "Is everyone agreed that this is a good location?"

Quick agreement, and why not. It was sheltered from severe weather, and very well camouflaged. If you weren't looking for the site, you'd go right by it and never notice.

Going home was much, much easier, with Thunder to help. The snow was too soft and deep for the Fliffs to walk on, but Thunder's long legs and remarkable power made it easy for him to march through the snow and pull the toboggan and its six passengers.

When they reached the oak tree and bushes where the Zebras were hidden, Father sent the children to check that the snow garage was in good condition and Moonseeker nice and dry.

Once the children were poking around in the bushes, it was conference time for the Fliff seniors and Thunder.

"So," Father said softly, "do you see any problems? I mean real problems?"

"No," Thunder replied. "If you can soften the frozen ground, I can definitely continue the excavation work. And I know where we can get a 'shell', as Charles calls it. Not far from here, as a matter of fact. Is there something else? Betsy, I detect an expression of concern. Would you tell me about it?"

Betsy nodded slowly. She felt very much at ease, speaking of this difficult matter to the Dog. "I'm worried about the People," she said. "If we go through with this, life will change. We love our Two-Leg family and we don't want them to worry. Fred, how do you feel about this?"

"Pretty much the same as you, dear. About the Williams, I mean. However, as I discovered when I was on that mountain and scared I might fall a million miles, when I was back home safe and sound, I knew that life had changed. You gave us an Idea, Betsy, when you wanted to reach higher. And now we have become partners with Ideas. We have gone into the sky and down the Hill because of Ideas. We have met our friend Thunder..."

"And that terrible predator, Hunter," Mother added quickly.

"Oh indeed," Father continued. "Risk is a partner of Change. But I am confident that we will work out another plan about our Two-Leg family. What do you think, Thunder?"

The big Dog looked out over the Hill. He took a deep breath and frowned. He was thinking. Finally he spoke.

"Our kind became partners with Two-Legs many, many years ago. We have been good partners to them, Fred. Very loyal, very protective. And most People have been kind to us. But too many of our kind lead uninteresting lives now. We are happiest when we work and when we are part of a family. The way it is now, too many Two-legs think it would be wonderful to have a nice big Dog..."

Thunder paused. He lifted his majestic head. A sad tear fell to the ground.

"Yes, like me," he went on. "But so often they just lose interest in us. Then we don't get enough exercise and they ignore us and that is when our kind begins to act out. We want so much to work, and to protect them and be good company and be part of the family..."

Thunder had to stop. He took several deep, shuddering breaths. Fred and Betsy could tell that their dear friend was very distressed, but there was nothing they could do, except get close to their very own Dragon and pat the top of his huge paw.

He looked down at them. He winked and slowly grinned. Finally Thunder had recovered.

"The Williams are good Creatures. I do some patrol work with Mr. Williams and they take me on walks quite often. But I take my own trips from time to time, too. Sometimes for a day or two, and they don't seem to worry. That is the big issue, isn't it? We do not want our People families to worry about us.

"That is rather a long answer, I'm afraid," Thunder continued. "I am loyal to my family, just as you are. But I agree with your thesis, Fred. We have an Idea and we must try it. If you wish to continue, I will work with you. I can collect the shell when you're ready. In fact, I might need a young helper. Any suggestions?"

Thunder spotted Charlie, struggling through the deep snow to rejoin them. Charlie had heard what Thunder just said about a helper.

"It should be I," Charlie spoke up firmly and correctly. "I know the design."

Thunder looked back to Charlie's parents, to see what their reaction would be. They were grinning proudly; they trusted their younger lad. Thunder liked that about the Fliffs. Courage and confidence. So many Creatures these days seemed to have abandoned those vital qualities of character.

CHAPTER 29

COLLECTING PARTS

"That's the shell? ZOW—EEE!" Charlie shouted, as he did a cartwheel on the road adjacent to the construction site.

It was the next night and Charlie and Thunder were together, on a road north of the Williams' property. Thunder waited until Charlie was finished with his enthusiastic gymnastics. "Exactly so," he said. "That is the shell, as you call it. There's nothing wrong, I hope."

"Absolutely not. Thunder, it's A-one perfect! The size is just right and it looks plenty strong. What was that... I guess it's a pipe, huh? Or a big cylinder... what's it for, do you know?"

The pipe, or cylinder, or 'shell', was in a 'Trash' area for recycled materials, off to the side of the excavation. The construction work was almost done. A large trench had been dug alongside the road, leaving piled up snow with plenty of dirt mixed in, and a new culvert. The digging machine, a backhoe, was sitting quietly alongside.

But it was that big item in the trash that had Charlie so excited. The pipe. It looked enormous. Next to the section of culvert pipe were the remains of a giant spool. The two end pieces of the spool had also caught Charlie's attention. He asked Thunder what that spool was, or had been.

"That was another type of cylinder, Charles. For holding cable," Thunder replied. "That was a word the workers used--'cable'. The workers unrolled cable from the spool, as you call it, and pulled the cable through long white tubes. Then they filled the dirt back in. You can see left-over pieces of tube over there."

"Well, you certainly hit the jackpot. Those ends will save us a lot of time. But..." Charlie paused. "You know," he continued, "as I look at this pile, I'm kind of worried about something."

"I can tell by your expression," Thunder said. "I see worry written in your eyebrows. Perhaps we can solve the problem together."

"You betcha," said the young Fliff. "See, if we take the spool pieces away, tomorrow morning when they start work again, the workers will probably notice something's missing. Then they might decide to recycle everything before other stuff disappears."

"Like the section of pipe they cut off because it was too long."

Charlie gave the big Dog a thumbs-up. "Egg-zactly."

Thunder stood and looked around. Then he went to the railing by the culvert and got up on his hind legs, so he could see even farther.

Then he got down and returned to the trash area.

"Your concern is very reasonable. You believe it would be best to move everything—the pipe *and* the end pieces from the spool—tonight."

Charlie had been re-measuring the cylinder, as best he could reach. "Yes, sir," he said, "I do."

"Very good. Here is my suggestion. We can hook a line to the pipe and you and I will pull it over to those pines, where we can hide it." Thunder gestured with his large head. "Then we will drag brush over the tracks in the snow..."

"Like you did before, to cover our tracks."

"Very good, Charles. We can come back another evening to get the pipe. I'm going to need your help. Once we get back here from the pines, we will tie a tow line to the spool pieces and make a bee line to our own construction site on Big Hill. The team can decide how to use them.

"Now, Charles, this is going to be a lot of work. Are you up to the job?" Thunder asked, knowing full well that the Fliffs would agree to move the moon, if he asked them to.

"You bet, sir."

It was more easily agreed upon than done. The large pipe section could not be skidded—too big and too heavy. Although the Fliffs were very inventive, this time it was Thunder who figured out how to move the piece. By rolling it! He had Charlie make a big V with the tow line while he put a long stick through the pipe, like an axle. Then he asked Charlie to tie the top part of the V to each end of the axle, while he held the bottom of the V so he could pull it.

Success! This contraption didn't roll fast, but it did roll and the Trash Raiders managed to pull the large cylinder across the road and up a slight hill into a thick pine stand. Thunder propped some pine boughs in front of it, for camouflage. Amazingly, that did the trick. Unless you knew precisely where to look, you would never spot the culvert pipe hidden in the pines.

Disguising the track was relatively easy. Thunder pulled Charlie, who sat on a small board. Charlie held a pine bough that he squiggled back and forth in the snow to disturb the soft snow around the track. Not perfect, but the odd marks disguised the track that had been left by the rolling cylinder.

The next job was the real Biggie—towing the two end pieces all the way back to Big Hill. Charlie fashioned a harness out of rope. He padded it so the harness wouldn't chafe the Dog's neck. The other end was wrapped around the two spool pieces, and this time it was Charlie who came up with a clever scheme to make the towing easier.

Using a piece of scrap aluminum they found in the trash pile, they made a rounded bumper to fit *under* the tow line in *front* of the pieces, so the package would slide like a sled on top of the snow.

Before they left, Charlie collected several lengths of scrap tubing and off they went. Charlie had learned the fine art of scavenging from the expeditions to find parts for the Elevator and Moonseeker.

Charlie rode on Thunder's neck, so he could keep track of the 'sled' and the harness.

It was quite a journey. Going across open field, they sang songs of adventure, of animals great and small, of mountains and rivers, of jungles and of soaring in the skies. Charlie, usually shy, was surprised at how relaxed he was about singing the Songs of Pig Survival. Thunder encouraged the lad.

With his long, strong legs, the Wolfhound kept up a good pace and showed few signs of fatigue. Not even going uphill. On the one steep section, he did have to stop once to catch his breath, but otherwise he moved steadily.

Downhill travel was a different matter. Here, Charlie jumped onto the 'sled' and pushed a braking pole into the snow until Thunder had a chance to turn around, so that *he* was uphill and the pieces were below him. That way Thunder could hold the sled back, so it wouldn't slide down the hill out of control. Charlie was astonished that the Wolfhound could hold the tow line... now the braking line... in his teeth and powerful jaws. Charlie was very glad that he was friendly with the owner of those teeth.

. Two and one-half long, hard hours later the Trash Raider Duo arrived at the new secret construction site on the side of Big Hill. Everyone was so happy to be together again. Especially Mother and Father. Charlie and Thunder had been away for three and one-half hours. They had been a little worried, but evidently Charlie hadn't been. He was chattering like a Blue Jay as he described the huge scavenging trip.

The Fliffs were delighted when they saw what superb goodies the team had salvaged. Charlie told them about the pipe cylinder and how the spool pieces would fit. His family was very impressed. If they fit together as Charlie had described, it would save them a whole lot of effort.

They worked for another hour, to complete the digging. Then they piled snow over the materials and concealed the site entrance as best possible. The Team of Seven did great work, but it sure was a tired team that headed back to their People homes.

Thunder gave them long tow rides up the Hill and across the lawn. When asked if he was tired, Thunder said that he was having so much fun, tired couldn't catch him. He seemed to have an endless supply of energy and good will.

Later, after Mother and Father had helped the children get back up to the balcony, Mother stopped Fred. "I don't know if you noticed," she said, "but Thunder had a couple of raw spots on his shoulders. They looked painful. And he had a small cut on his left hind leg. He wouldn't let me do a thing, but Oyster went right up to him..."

Mother paused, to blink back a tear of pride.

"...and our caring, brave little child said to that beautiful huge Dog, 'Now you lie down right now and let me clean those *in-jerries*. I don't want you to get an *inspection*.'" Mother sniffed.

Father laughed. "She said that, '*inspection*'? And he went along with it?" He laughed again.

"He certainly did. Fred, you have no idea how big he is, and how gentle. When she rubbed the medicine onto the raw spot, I could tell it hurt. But Oyster asked him if it hurt, and he said, 'Not a bit. It feels like a new shoulder.' And he thanked her."

"What about the cut?"

"I looked at it. It seemed clean, but I told Thunder that there would be no Expedition tomorrow night."

"And he went along with that, too?"

"Well, certainly, dear."

Father shook his head and laughed again. He imagined his wife and daughter telling a Lion what to do... and the Lion saying 'Okay'. What a team.

Then, for the first time, Father had a picture in his mind precisely what their project would look like when it was complete. What an Idea!

CHAPTER 30

WINTER CONSTRUCTION

The Fliffs had seen Thunder dig holes in the snow, and they were always astonished at how much snow he could move. Now they were seeing him again and it truly was a sight to behold. The magnificent huge Dog got those front paws going and it was like a cyclone hitting a snowdrift. The snow flew! In seconds he was down two feet and in two minutes he had dug a trench in the snow seven feet long.

"I guess he feels fully recovered from the other night," Father said, standing back a little so he wouldn't be blanketed in flying snow.

Mother was just as amazed. The children were, too. All of them watched the excavation and thanked their lucky stars that *they* didn't have to clear away the snow.

Thunder had the snow-clearing job done in less than a half hour. Before you could say Big Dog Biscuit ten times, there it was, a large patch of exposed dry grass and frozen ground, ready for the next stage of work. "Is that about what you want?" he asked.

"Excellent," Rhoda said. "What a big help you are, Thunder. We'll start the fire right there."

The other Fliffs were already dragging pieces of dry wood and kindling to the area Rhoda had pointed to. Sherman had cleared a path to the closest pine tree, so they could gather twigs and branches. The Fliffs were going to try a "Hot Coals Excavation Method", which would work like this:

Because the ground was frozen, it had to be thawed before they could begin digging. They did this by building a campfire over a patch of frozen ground and waiting for the heat to thaw the frost.

When the fire had burned down quite a bit, using green pusher sticks, the Fliffs would push the hot coals over to a new spot (very carefully), add more dry wood, and begin to dig where the ground had been warmed and thawed.

It took a bit of experimenting to get the fire big enough to warm the ground, but not so big as to be dangerous.

The thawing technique worked, but it was slow going. Slow *and* dirty. After an hour of hard work, Rhoda measured the hole and calculated that twenty-seven percent of the digging had been done.

"And," she added, pointing at her calculations, "the *last* twenty-three percent of the digging will be *much* slower because we'll be deeper and everything will have to be hauled up with *buckets*. That's the bad news."

Everyone groaned—they knew that Rhoda was usually right. Then Charlie spoke up. "Wait. You said 'bad' news. You got any good news for us?"

Rhoda smiled at her brother, and nodded. "Sure, Chaz. The first good news is, I won't correct your careless grammar. The second good news is, we've dug down below the frost line. This means we won't have to do the warm-fire-and-coals routine anymore. Cool, huh?"

This time the others didn't bother to groan at Rhoda's joke. Or laugh. Just deep sighs at the promise of heavy lifting ahead. The soft sound of sighs signaled Mother that everyone needed a Pick-Me-Up. So, out came the goodies knapsack—

time for a nice tea and snack break. The Fliffs had packed two extra biscuits for Thunder, as well as a much larger cup.

After they had snacked and rested, Father asked if everyone wanted to go back to work for an hour. The answer was a resounding YES!

"Good," he said. "I trust Rhodie's calculations. I figure it will take us two more sessions like tonight's to get the pit deep enough. You agree?" he asked Rhoda.

She nodded.

Father brushed some dirt off his face and managed to make a big black soot smear across his cheek. Oyster laughed. Father looked at her. "Well," he said, "you don't want me wearing dirt in my whiskers, do you?"

With that, he wiped again, with more of the same result and more laughter. Even Thunder could not help himself. As he chuckled, he happened to glance down at his front paws and lo and behold, he was wearing Sooty Dog Gloves.

That was all it took for all seven diggers to smudge themselves silly, pointing at each other, laughing hysterically, and looking as though they had all taken a bath in ink. Luckily the soot more or less came off by scrubbing with snow, but for sure they had some additional work to do before returning home.

They worked another hour, the Fliffs tending the Keep-Warm fire and digging, while Thunder got wood and used a large branch to fluff up the snow where he had left tracks. Now that they were below the frost line, digging went a little faster.

Next evening's work went even faster, for one big reason: Thunder was able to work in the pit, because the Fliffs had come up with a scheme to remove dirt more quickly. By putting the tarp *in* the pit, Thunder could kick dirt onto it (and when he kicked dirt, piles of dirt **moved**). When a good pile had been deposited *on* the tarp, it was rolled up into a secure bundle and pulled *out of the pit* by ropes. Quite clever.

Progress the second night was so good, in fact, that at the end of the evening, while they all relaxed and sipped the last of the tea, Rhoda made a suggestion.

"From here on," she said, looking around and making mental calculations, "we will be deepening the pit and adding the special trenches. All that work will be digging and hauling. We can do that. Maybe you could get the cylinder, Thunder? Will that job take long?" she asked the Wolfhound.

He thought about it, making a picture in his head of the territory between the pines trees and where they were now. "Two hours, Rhoda," he finally said. "The cylinder is loose and ready to roll. I will need a helper, to fasten the rope."

Rhoda had an idea. Although she did not actually want to *say* it, the truth was that Oyster wasn't much help as a digger. She talked too much, for one thing. For another, she wasn't very skillful at helping to haul the dirt-filled tarp up. Eureka, Rhoda had a brainstorm. There was Thunder's helper!

"I think I can spare someone to help you," Rhoda said to the Dog. "It's possible you might get back here *before* the pit is big enough. Could you park the cylinder while we finished digging?"

"I believe so. The tow line would hold it."

Rhoda was about to ask about lowering the shell, when Sherman spoke up. He was in charge of Construction Scheduling.

"Alright, here's what I think," Sherman said. "We need another evening with all of us right here, to do the warming fire and digging. On the work session after that, the digging work will go quickly but there'll be lots of measuring and fiddling. Why don't four of us stay here for that work while you retrieve the cylinder, Thunder. If Rhodie agrees, we could send along *two* helpers. Once the cylinder is in place, we'll have to drop the end pieces in. Can you help us with that job, too?"

"Easy as apple pie, Master Sherman."

Rhoda and Sherman spoke together, made a few notes on the Plan, and there was more discussion, nods, frowns, and calculations.

Thunder enjoyed watching all of this. He did not get the chance to plan activities with other Dogs. But he did have Ancestral Memories of how his ancestors solved problems in the ancient past. He had an image of Wolves (who looked a lot like Wolfhounds, in Thunder's imagination) in a cave, sitting around a big campfire and discussing plans for tomorrow.

The Fliffs finally came to a conclusion about the schedule, which they presented to Thunder for approval. If he agreed, all of them would all dig for another hour, then cover up the site and go home. Tomorrow all of them would work as hard as they could. On the *third* night Thunder would collect his two helpers (great suspense about who would go with Oyster) and haul the cylinder from its hiding place in the pines to the site. Then, all seven of them would lower the end pieces into place and that would be that for a couple of days, so they could get some proper rest. Agreed?

Enthusiastic agreement!

Before starting work again, Mother said, "We figured that out pretty quickly. Did we forget something? Are we taking any risky chances?"

"Of course not," Father declared. "We know what we're doing, don't we? Of course we do," he said, answering his own question.

Everyone pretty much agreed that they had thought of everything. Mother was worried they might have missed a detail, and Sherman considered it, as did Rhodie. It sounds okay, they said.

But of course, Mr. Careful himself, Charlie, knew they were overlooking something. *Don't worry so much, Chaz,* someone said. *What's to get messed up? Thunder will be in charge of one crew and the rest of us will be working in the hole.*

So they shrugged off that last little doubt of Charlie's. That was a mistake. You know why? Because they had overlooked the most obvious and most likely source of mess-ups. Guess what... or who.

CHAPTER 31

THUNDER and HELPERS

As Thunder loped across the big field, he gulped great quantities of the cool, clean, night air. He loved going out at night. He loved to run and go sight-seeing, and when he found friendly Creatures who were not afraid of him, it was always a pleasure to stop and chat. There were so many interesting things to learn.

Take Birds, for example. Some of the Flying Creatures actually migrated half-way around the World. Some of the smallest fliers came from distant lands and made a trip back and forth every Sixth Moon or so! They spoke very casually about those long trips, but Thunder couldn't help being amazed at those tiny Birds being able to get through strong winds and heavy rains.

The Great Hawks mostly lived around here, but they were able to fly so high they could see distant mountains. One Owl he had spoken to, a large and impressive fellow feathered all in white, told Thunder about seeing glaciers!

Then there was a tiny Bird whose wings beat so fast they made a noise like a Bumble Bee. This plucky wee Being spent his entire day going from flower to flower. Ducks and Geese were great travelers, too, and when they spoke, everyone in the Forest could hear them.

Thunder had spoken briefly with a Bear. It was a Mother Bear and she warned Thunder not to harm her Cubs. Of course I wouldn't, he reassured her, and he added that she should pay the same courtesy to his People family. He didn't say *Or else*, but she understood.

On one occasion he had a conversation with a Snake. On a warm spring day Thunder was climbing on some big rocks when he heard a rattling noise that sounded very unpleasant. He stopped immediately, first as a cautionary measure, and secondly to investigate. To his surprise, it was a Snake whose tail actually made that rattling noise.

Evidently Rattler Snake could not hear, but he could *sense* other Creatures by the scent of their bodies, by vibrations that traveled on the ground, and by the heat their bodies gave off. That was how Snake found Creatures at night. (Thunder did not ask why Snake might be seeking other Creatures at night, but he made an educated guess.) The Snake, realizing that the Dog meant no harm, rattled its tail, then shook its head. Thunder understood. This was a warning: **Do not tread on me, please.** Thunder nodded, to indicate that he would always be careful.

What fine adventures those had been. But Thunder had to admit that for fun and inventiveness, nothing could surpass these furry little Pigs. They laughed at themselves, they loved other Creatures, and goodness, how about that flying machine and the racing sleds. Oh, yes, and an elevator made from a coffee can!

Thunder laughed again when he thought of that night when Fred appeared at his front door, dangling and twisting at the end of a piece of string, wearing a can.

These friends were not built for speed or power, but when you needed Ideas, all you had to do was look at a Guinea Pig and you could tell instantly that Great Ideas were being built in that fine mind.

Certainly the Hill Mystery Project was a Great Idea. Thunder was enjoying the nights of digging and the enthusiastic company of his small friends. He was also looking forward to tonight's big adventure—retrieving the culvert pipe and seeing it drop into the hole they had dug.

Thunder had arrived at the Williams' back lawn early. He settled himself by the tree where he could watch the balcony. He wanted to see the Small Pigs come zipping out. They were such fun to watch. It might be useful for him to be there, too. Even though Hunter the Cat had been warned, Thunder thought it was wise to double-check. You never knew whether Cats took a warning seriously or not.

Oops, there it was. The train—the Midnight Special. That was the signal to meet. Thunder looked up at the house and waited.

There they are on the balcony. Then lines dropped over the railing, and down they came. He was astonished to see how fast they rappelled. (A word they taught him.) Then into the shadows, then there they were again, scurrying across the snow, headed for the Juniper bush. They reminded Thunder of leaves that skittered across a lawn in a storm.

Before he knew it, suddenly out from under the bush came those zoomy Zebra sleds. Quick as quicksilver the two teams were ready and waiting for him at the top of the Hill. Thunder joined them. It took him four bounds to go from the back yard to the top of the Hill.

Now at the Project site and the snow cleared away again, Thunder examined what the Fliffs had made. It's a saddle, they said.

"Goodness, it is very impressive," he said. "Such good stitchery. Did you buy it at an expensive Saddle store?" He knew the Fliffs had made it, but a bit of flattery was well earned.

"We *made* it!" Oyster squeaked with pride. "That's where I ride and over there's where Charlie will ride. And see? Here's some nice soft cloth so it won't hurt your back. I needled that on myself."

Thunder leaned way down. "Oh yes," he said. "I recognize your careful work. That was very thoughtful. Will you help me get it on? We have miles to go and work to do before we dig." So saying, he lay down carefully and waited for someone to toss the strap over his back. Yup, there it was, and quick as a blink, he felt hands at his other side, pulling the strap.

"Could you lift your rib cage?" Father asked. "I need to push the strap underneath, so Mother can tie it."

Thunder did as requested. When Fred pushed the strap through, he patted the Dog, either as a way to signal Thanks, or as a way to tell Thunder where he was, just in case Thunder decided to roll over. The Fliffs thought of everything. Almost everything.

"I'm going to tighten the saddle strap now," Mother called. "Let me know if it's uncomfortable."

Breathing deeply, to see if it was too tight, Thunder felt no restriction. "Seems just right, Betsy. Are my passengers ready?"

"O... kay," a shaky voice said.

Thunder felt someone climb up. "O... kay, Mister Thunder."

"Do you want me to roll a bit?" Thunder asked.

"I'll try climbing up," Charlie said, "and then down the other side. Please don't move, sir. I'm not very comfortable with heights."

Thunder nearly laughed. "Steady as he goes," he said.

After a bit of cautious climbing and holding on, both young passengers were in.

"Hang on," Thunder said over his shoulder, "I'm going to stand up now."

Thunder heard two sets of squeaks when he stood up. But then a cautious "Wow" from one side, and ""My eyes are closed" from the other side. Brave little tykes, he thought.

Looking down at the four Fliffs, Thunder detected the expression of concern on the parents' faces. "The saddle feels secure," he said in a gentle voice, "and I am comfortable. Are we all ready?"

Mother and Father nodded to him. Thunder winked. He knew how they felt. "Trust me," he said. "We will have a calm trip and before you know it, that big pipe will be in the hole, ready for the end pieces. Are you comfortable, passengers? Hanging on?"

Two Yeses.

"Permission to go?" Thunder asked.

The Wolfhound's deep voice and confident manner did a lot to reassure Mother and Father. They knew that their friend would protect the children at all cost. Mother smiled bravely, and in a voice that tried to sound casual, she called up, "Careful journey, all."

Father gave them a jaunty *Thumbs Up*, the way a ground crew would signal the pilot of those fabulous P-38 Lightnings he had seen on TV.

"Tally ho," Thunder called.

"Fliffs away," the two riders called together.

"Calm and steady," Sherman called up.

Days later, when Father thought about Thunder leaving that night on the pipe retrieval mission with his two children, he recalled his reaction when Sherman had called up "Calm and steady" to the crew. 'Calm and steady?' Father had said to himself. When Oyster was involved? Ha! Not a chance.

Father was more right than he could ever have imagined.

CHAPTER 32

DIGGING, SAVING TIME

They don't call Guinea Pigs "Ground Beavers" for nothing. Digging and sculpting the raw Earth is second nature to GPs, and as soon as they reached the Secret Site on the Hill, they removed the camouflage tarp and began to finish the Big Dig.

This one was going to be completed exactly on, or before, schedule. There was only one major chore left: Removing a large rock. The plan had been to save that task for Thunder, but because he was away, retrieving the culvert pipe, the Digging Team figured they could get rid of the rock themselves.

Father was pushing the rock with all his strength, and he had managed to roll the heavy thing partway up to the sloping exit ramp. But he couldn't get the rock all the way to the top. It was too heavy. Through clenched, gleaming white teeth he called out: "QUICK... someone jam... something, anything under this monster. HURRY," he grunted.

Rhoda, who was closest, grabbed the nearest object and wedged it under the rock. Father let go of the rock, but before he had a chance to sigh with relief, there was an ugly-sounding 'C-r-u-n-c-h' and a 'S-q-u-o-o-s-h' and the rock rolled all the way back to its original resting place at the bottom of the hole.

Luckily, the rolling stone gathered no injuries on its dash back home. However, once re-parked, it inflicted a minor injury when Father gave it an angry kick.

"OW" Father grunted. "OW, Ow ow! That hurt."

Everyone waited until Father's rosy disposition returned. It took a minute or two, but then there he was, wincing a little but smiling.

"Now," he said, in the cheeriest voice he could manage, "Rhodie, dear, what was *that*?" Pointing at a mashed, crumpled black bag.

"This?" she asked timidly, holding up a flattened knapsack. Sherman, of course, had seen all this. He was about to laugh at Rhodie for using a *knapsack* to hold back a huge stone, when he remembered what had been *inside* the knapsack. Wouldn't you know it? Only moments before, Sherman had been thinking about a snack. Mom had packed grapes, beet stems, and wheat biscuits, all of which he loved. Sherman grabbed the flattened knapsack from Rhoda and pried it open.

Oh, brother. The grapes were now grape jelly, the beet stems were stringy, red unknowns, and the glorious brown wheat biscuits were still brown, but in a million small pieces. His extra pair of white socks looked as though they had taken a trip through a sloppy paint factory and his gloves looked like something Kenny Knuckles, the Clown, would wear.

"This was my *L-U-N-C-H!*" he howled.

Luckily, that drama played out pretty quickly when Rhoda managed to change the subject by mentioning that Thunder and the culvert pipe would be arriving soon. Down went the collapsed sack and up went the shovels. Changing the subject always worked.

They solved the rock problem by digging a long trench from the boulder to the edge of the dig. It rolled out quite easily in the trench, and kept going down the Hill until it hit the pond, broke the ice, and sank. The rock-and-roll technique worked. Maybe it had a future.

An hour later, they were digging away and getting into a nice rhythm with the shovels and tarp, when they all heard a muffled **BANG** far off in the distance.

Goodness," Mother exclaimed, looking up. "Could that be thunder? The sky kind, I mean?"

"Maybe a truck going over the Old Bridge," Father suggested.

Now it was Sherman's turn. "I think it was a sonic boom. An SR-71 Blackbird." (He was a big fan of high performance aircraft.)

All of them were incorrect. Luckily they didn't know what the noise had been. Thunder knew, and wished he didn't.

Very quickly, Oyster lost her nervousness about riding way up high. Thunder could tell, because she wasn't clinging to his coat so tightly. He was glad. "Are you ready for some speed?" he called out.

"LET'S GO," Oyster yelled into the wind.

"Master Charles?"

"FULL SPEED," Charlie replied, which was bold for him.

Go they did, and nearly at full speed. Thunder's long legs made rapid work of the country miles on the cleared road. The passengers got a surprise when he leapt over a snow bank into a field, but then Charlie remembered that the cylinder was hidden in the pine trees.

When they arrived, Thunder pulled the camouflage pine boughs away from the big cylinder. It sure was big! Oyster said "Wowie!"

Thunder explained the procedure for using the tow line, and it would be more complicated this time because, besides going up and down hills, which would require help from the passenger-helpers, they would have to steer the cylinder, too.

When he was through explaining, Oyster said, "What will we do if a car comes along? I mean won't the person be really su'prised to see a great big metal thing rolling along with us three *Tree-chures*?"

Both Thunder and Charlie were 'su'prised'. It took Chaz a few seconds to figure out what 'Tree-chures' were. (Creatures.) Thunder really did a double-take. "Car? Person?" he said. Then he understood what she meant.

"Don't worry, young Fliff. We won't be using the road. It would be faster, I agree with you, but far too risky. No, my friend, we are going through the Forest. You should find that very interesting."

Charlie's heart sank. He had heard a lot about the Forest... a lot of bad things. In his imagination the Forest was a dark, mysterious Kingdom. Behind every tree was a huge Cat... or a Bear... and on every big rock sat a Wolf or Coyote or even Big Foot. (He didn't know much about this fellow, but he sounded extremely menacing.)

Oyster, on the other hand, had complete faith in Thunder. Worried about the Forest? Who, me worry?

"Do we got to?" Charlie asked.

"What's that?"

"Go through the Forest?"

Thunder could tell that the lad was worried, and he remembered that on some of their evenings together, he had told the Fliff family about going on patrol through the Forest. Hmmm-m. He pondered a minute.

"Well," he said, "we could go around. It will take longer..." Thunder paused, hoping Charlie would change his mind. Or perhaps young Oyster would scold him for being cautious.

No luck. Silence from his companions and helpers.

"All right, then. Hitch me up, you two. The roundabout way it is. And we begin with this hill." Thunder gestured with his big paw.

Thunder made sure the tow line was properly tied, and it would be easier this time, because the saddle strap was also a harness for towing. The Fliffs had thought of everything. So, when all was set, and the helpers knew what to do when Thunder had to stop to rest, off they went.

It was slow going. The snow was softer now, and the hill steeper. Thunder worked hard, pulling that section of culvert pipe, and he had to stop more often than he had expected. But he kept at it.

The very first leg of the trek took a half-hour.

At the top, Thunder sat down, took a deep breath, and laid out the situation: "At this rate the trip will take four hours. Or more. You can see where we're going." He gestured toward more hills in the distance. "If we make good progress it will be nearly dawn when we get to the secret construction site. *Another* possibility is to stop halfway and begin again tomorrow. What do you think?"

Charlie, who paid close attention, said, "I could tell by the way you said *another* that there's a third choice. What's that?"

Shrugging, so it wouldn't be too obvious that the third choice was his favorite, Thunder said, casually, "Well, I go into the Forest quite often and I have no trouble there. We could go that way and save a bunch of time. It is up to you, my friends. You decide."

They did, but not instantly. Oyster was amazingly, for her, very logical and persuasive. She said it wasn't fair for Thunder to do all that work. And if it snowed tomorrow, there would be so-o-o-o much extra work. She said that *she* wasn't a bit scared of the Forest. "Of course, Charlie, if you're gonna..."

Charlie knew what was coming. She was going to say "...be a baby about it."

"Oh all right." Charlie said.

Having surrendered to his sister, Charlie had an idea for getting through the Forest more quickly. He explained it.

"We can roll the pipe. See, the hill to the Forest isn't steep. We untie the cylinder and just steer it a little."

"It's grabity," Oyster piped up.

"What?" Charlie asked.

"You know what I mean. When things fall. I read about it."

"Gravity—with a *V*, Oyster. Not '*grabity*'. You oughta read more carefully."

Oyster was going to say something smart, but she couldn't think of anything. Darn that Charlie. Always smarter than anyone else.

"The Forest route it is, then," declared the Wolfhound. "Here we go. This will be a lot quicker and much more exciting."

Thunder was certainly right about that!
Unfortunately.

CHAPTER 33

OYSTER'S WILD RIDE

Rolling the great big culvert pipe was kind of fun. On level ground where the snow wasn't deep, Thunder could roll it just by pushing with his front paws. Seeing how that huge cylinder rolled along, Oyster asked Thunder if she and Charlie could run on top of the cylinder.

Before the enormous Dog even had a chance to reply, Charlie declined. "Not for me, thanks," Charlie said. Running high up like that, on top of a very large cylinder, did not strike him as a keen plan.

"I'm afraid that answer applies to you, too," Thunder said to Oyster. "If you slip and the culvert pipe rolls on top of you, I don't dare think what might happen."

"Okay," she said. "I totally understand."

When Charlie heard that, a little alarm bell went off inside his nobly shaped head—his sister agreeing? And so quickly? Hmmm, *that* sure didn't sound right. But the thought didn't last long. Ahead was the dark Forest and Charlie was dubious about going through there. But, seeing no monsters directly ahead, Charlie's interest shifted back to the long journey home.

As for Thunder, he felt very content. Meeting this strange little family of thinkers and adventurers had been a tonic for him. He liked their silliness, too. They were jolly good company.

Wrapped in these pleasant thoughts, and with the cylinder moving so nicely toward the top of the hill, Thunder didn't detect that his littlest passenger had climbed out of her saddle and slid to the ground on a line. Why would he notice that? Oyster didn't weigh much, so it wasn't as if the load had suddenly lightened. Plus, the cylindrical pipe made a crunchy noise in the snow, as it was being pushed.

Then when Thunder turned to the right, to say something to Charlie, why would he notice that the *other* Fliff had darted ahead and had jumped *into* the rolling cylinder? Besides which, Thunder wasn't really familiar with Oyster's magnetic attraction to getting in trouble. So, why on earth would he have the slightest inkling that the littlest Fliff was now Outside and not in the grip of his immediate protection?

As dangerous as the situation had become, poor Thunder was completely innocent and unsuspecting.

Naturally, Oyster had not given one single thought to the possibility that she might be in peril. All she knew was what fun she was having.

At first Oyster lay on her side and let the cylinder gently tumble her like a bundle of clothes in a slow dryer. Then she tried doing hand-stands, then somersaults. That was so fabulous she thought, *Gosh, I always wanted to jog,* so she tried that, too. To her surprise, she could run faster than the shell rolled. **Wowser ka-zootie**!

Oyster was having such a good time that now *she* failed to detect something important happening. The cylinder was rolling a little faster and—*very* important clue—the sound of Dog nails on the metal had stopped. At first, Oyster didn't realize that the cylinder was rolling down the hill. By itself!

Thunder saw this, of course. The snow was a bit deeper here, so the pipe wasn't rolling very fast. That would give him plenty of time to run ahead and nudge it a little to the right or left before it crashed into some bushes. He told Charlie what he was doing.

"Great," Charlie said. "What're those other bushes? The tall ones."

"Blueberries, Charles."

"Real ones? The blue ones? The kind you eat? Amazing."

"It is. I enjoy them. Hold on... I have to nudge the cylinder again, Charles. Last chance before it's going too fast for us to keep up."

Thunder did just that, doing his best to point the cylinder toward clear passage on the left side of the Forest. Then it would be on its own.

Charlie held tight as Thunder sprang ahead. Charlie watched with amazement as the big Dog nudged the huge piece of cylindrical metal. Then he felt Thunder veer quickly to the side, to get out of the way. Away the pipe went. On its own.

Charlie called over, across the Wolfhound's powerful back: "Hey Oyster, how'd you like to be running on top of that thing now, huh? Bet you couldn't keep up."

He waited for a smarty remark.

"Hey Oyster, still want to surf the cylinder?"

No reply. He thought that was odd. Weird, in fact. "**Oy... ster**," he called, this time very seriously.

Thunder heard the alarm in the lad's voice and at that same instant, he realized there was no weight in Oyster's saddle. He skidded to a stop and turned his huge head as far as he could.

No Oyster*!*

An icicle of fear pierced his stomach. Although he was mortally afraid of what the answer would be, Thunder had to ask.

"Charles," he said, his deep voice trembling, "is your sister with you?"

The way he said it told Charlie that this wasn't a game. "No sir," he called. "She ain't."

(Youngsters sometimes forget proper grammar when they're concerned about something.)

Thunder felt a jolt of horror. This was worse than anything he could imagine. The child was missing! Quickly, he turned and looked back up at the track in the snow. Maybe... Oh please, **maybe** she'll be there, the silly little child, slogging through the snow, waving, all excited, and jabbering away.

But no.

Thunder could hardly speak. "Charles," he said, trying to sound normal, "I need a good idea in a *huge* hurry. Your sister is *not* with us and I do... not... know *where* she could be. We must start searching **immediately**. But I have *no idea where to begin*. Please, Charles, use that keen mind of yours. Where should I look? She needs us."

Charlie was so scared he was nearly sick to his stomach. He was a cautious Creature by nature, and the idea that his own sister might be lost... alone... scared... in this dark, cold, bleak wilderness gave him a dreadful sinking feeling. He could picture the dopey brat, alone, and calling out for him. *Charl... ie help me... e... e...*

'I gotta think!' he commanded himself. 'THINK Charlie!'

While Charlie's brain was whirring, Oyster was in the same boat, but worse. Her body was

206

whirring. She was tumbling so fast that she had lost track of up, down, and sideways. The cylinder was rolling w-a-a-a-y faster than she could keep up. She had lost all control. All! Trapped, in the cylinder of rolling steel.

Then, suddenly, in a flash of keen insight, Charlie knew where his sister was. The one place where Oyster most likely had gone.

"She's in the pipe!" he yelled. **"That's *gotta* be it!"**

The lad was right! Thunder stared in horror as the large cylinder rolled down the hill as if it were racing against the shadows of night.

There was no way he could catch it, let alone stop the runaway. Thunder had to close his eyes. He didn't want to see what was going to happen next. The cylinder was heading straight for a large clump of juniper bushes.

Thunder and Charlie watched helplessly as the cylinder went faster and faster, then hitting the juniper bush and making a tremendous noise: **W... W... Whum... pppp!** The cylinder bounced way up into the air.

Oyster, who just seconds ago had been frightened and sore, was startled when, all of a sudden, the rolling seemed to stop. The noise stopped. She seemed to be released from invisible ropes. But it was **not** a good feeling. Oh oh. Oyster knew what had happened. It was like in the Zebras, when they flew off a rock and sailed through the air. *Oh OH!* She braced for the landing.

Thunder and Charlie saw the whole thing. "Hang on, Charles," Thunder said over his shoulder. "And keep a brave hope."

The large metal cylinder landed with a **WH-H-H... OOOM**, then bounced. It hit a high-bush blueberry. **BOI... ING**, it bounced and turned and hit a nice little birch sapling that had been slumbering all winter. The out-of-control pipe spun off that and went on rolling, bouncing, and banging downhill. Up, down, around, down, over...

Would it go on like this forever? Would the wee small Guinea Pig inside be battered into a furry mess? Actually, the banging that Oyster experienced was painful, yes indeed, and sickening, and dizzying, but it did not cause terrible damage. The child was wearing a nice thick snowsuit, with a thick hood, and she had enough sense to curl into a tight ball. She was mightily confused, dizzy, and scared, but not injured.

Then the wild, out-of-control section of culvert pipe decided to give up this nonsensical trip. Well, actually, a tall, thin maple tree made the decision. It stood directly in the cylinder's path and braced itself for the crash. **Crash**. And stop.

What brought the poor, battered and banged Oyster back to her senses? Hard to say. An army of bruises was bragging, and her stomach was still doing gymnastic tumbles, and her head was ringing like a broken church bell.

But what probably caused her to wake up and pay attention? Pure Jungle Instinct. Oyster heard the most chilling, piercing, terrifying screech she had ever heard in her life. The ripping sound tore through the dark tunnel like a scorched banshee. Oyster's fur not only stood on end, it nearly jumped off her bruised brown body.

But the screech was not the worst of it. Nope! The worst was knowing what had **made** that noise. It was the *Call of the Predator,*

and the small child knew what Predators were. She had tried to attack a Predator that was threatening her family. The family carried Sun Bombs to scare Predators. She had heard Bert Williams talk about giant Lions and Tigers and Pythons. Little Pigs and Big Predators were not a good mix. And here, right here, was a... a....

Predator! She saw the thing. It walked into the cylinder.

Oyster tried to call for help but her throat was paralyzed. She froze.

The thing was tall and it seemed to fill the cylinder with the grim light of Doom. It had two horns and huge glowing, unblinking, green eyes. It opened its cape and the cape rustled like the dried leaves in a tomb. Then it screeched again.

The small Pig's small life passed before her eyes. She saw her sister flying near the moon, herself playing trapeze under the Balloons. Pop, with his funny, wise words, Sherm the smart guy, her buddy Chaz, Chloe and Bert, and of course, her new best pal, the gigantic beautiful big Wolfhound. She would miss them terribly. I loved you, she said silently.

Oyster heard the sharp whisper of a razor beak. It was closer now.

Calling upon the very last of her strength, Oyster yelled, in her sweet, high, terrified but brave voice,

"THUN... DER."

The *Plea for Help* flew out of the pipe and sped past the trees and bushes, twisting up and down on its way in a desperate search for her friend.

Then, as that cry had nearly lost its energy, having tried its very, very best to do its duty... then, at the last possible moment, the urgent cry reached its target. It seemed like a distant whisper, but Thunder heard her call his name and his heart filled with happiness. The child was alive! She needed help, but she was alive. And, as Great Animals can sense when friends are in trouble, Thunder knew that Oyster's life was being threatened. He called out for all to hear. It was the Wolfhound's answer to the child's call for help. The answer was so strong and clear that Forest and Field froze to listen. There would be no defying this call. It would be obeyed. The Law of Animals spoke:

"NO CREATURE SHALL HARM THE CHILD.

THUNDER SPEAKS."

The child did not remember the Owl leaving. She didn't remember when she saw the huge shadow of the Wolfhound at the mouth of the tunnel. Or the little figure running down the tunnel, (and falling once and getting right up). Oyster remembered looking up at the great white fangs and being so happy! She remembered his huge smile and his deep voice. She remembered the small, joyful voice of her brother, who was so tiny next to the Dog. Somehow, Oyster managed to cry with gratitude and kiss and hug a **small** brother and an **enormous** Dog at the same time.

Yes, Thunder had spoken. And he had been heard.

CHAPTER 34

HOME(S)

There are times when a scolding is not necessary. The mistake punishes itself and from it comes Wisdom. It is called a *Life Lesson* and aren't we grateful when we come out of the dark tunnel with only a few bruises... and are hugged by parents who know when not to scold.

The section of culvert pipe dropped into the excavated hole quite well, and snapping the end caps into place was only a small bit of extra effort to trim this and straighten that. The work crew took extra care to seal the seam between the end caps and the cylinder so that water would not leak in.

The biggest job was cutting openings for a stove chimney, a nice big door, and a ventilation duct. Listen to how Father explained ventilation to Thunder:

"Well, Thunder, um..mm... with seven of us in the cabin, we'll need ventilation. You know, so the air is fresh. The stove, too."

Thunder nodded and waited for more. Finally Sherman spoke up.

"When we breathe, we give off moisture and carbon dioxide. We have to get rid of those contaminants, otherwise the cabin wall would get wet and we'd have a harder and harder time breathing. Getting enough Oxygen to breathe is A-one important. We also need fresh air to supply the stove, so it will burn the wood nice and hot and the smoke will go up the chimney. If the stove didn't burn fast enough, a dangerous gas could leak into our new house."

"What kind of gas would that be?" Thunder inquired.

"Carbon mon... mon..."

"...monoxide," Rhoda filled in. "Carbon monoxide. And other stuff. But don't worry, Outside air flows through here pretty well because there's a breeze on the Hill and we cut those ventilation holes."

"Excellent explanations," Thunder said. "You Fliffs truly are quite ingenious. Show me how I can help."

"You already have," Mother said. "By finding the culvert section, and getting it here. That, plus the ends, gives us a cabin big enough for our family of seven."

Thunder understood the arithmetic and blushed and grinned proudly. No one could see him blush, but they certainly could see him grin.

So, while the Fliffs worked inside their cabin, they set Thunder to work outside, filling the dirt back in around the cabin and covering everything with snow and leaves. In front, where the door was, he piled brush and logs up against the dirt, leaving just enough room to get in and out. Several times as he worked, Thunder stopped and stepped back to take a careful look at the area where their cabin was hidden. Better and better. Except for the paw prints in the snow (which they could brush away) their secret cabin was practically invisible.

Work was going well inside, too. The Fliffs installed hooks to hang Moonseeker up and out of the way, and soon enough they would bring the Zebras down here. In a week or two there would be shelves and cabinets and hooks to store and hang things, such as dry clothes and cups and books and water and their flashlights. There were small tins and glass jars for storing special food treats. Eventually they would bring in dried apples and pears, biscuits, wheat germ, and all manner of goodies. There was a special large bag for Thunder's chow. (And of course he shared their food—but not more than a tiny morsel.)

Hooking up the small stove was easy enough. They used this mostly to warm the interior when they first arrived, and to drive off any moisture. The stove was dandy for heating tea, too.

By the third week, the Fliffs and Thunder had brought certain tools and materials to the cabin. Thunder had asked them to do this, because he wanted the Fliffs to make a saddle with enough room for all of them. At one point, when the saddle was laid out on the floor for double-stitching, Oyster looked at it, at her family, and then at Thunder.

"Wow," she exclaimed. "That's pretty big! Can you carry us... all of us? Won't you get tired? Where're we goin', Mr. Thunder?"

The huge Dog smiled. "If I get tired," he replied, "I know you won't mind walking. Where we're going is a Secret. I promise, you'll enjoy it."

When the saddle was finished and properly adjusted, and when the snow was mostly melted, Thunder announced one night that it was time for the Mystery ride. The Fliffs were excited. Faster than a speeding idea, they attached the new saddle to the big Dog and climbed up to it.

"Everyone comfortable?" Thunder called over his powerful shoulders.

"You bet" and "Yessir" came the replies.

"Holding on?"

Same replies.

"Off we go, then," the huge Dog announced. "It is time for introductions."

No one knew what he was talking about, but the aura of excitement was shimmering like the Northern Lights. This was going to be... Wow!

Sherman dismounted so he could close the cabin door, then climbed back up, and off they went at full gallop. My Oh My, how Thunder could fly! In only minutes, so it seemed, speeding through the night, the six Pigs and the Wolfhound crossed broad fields and shallow streams and in a trice they were at the entrance to the Forest. The Great Forest.

Oddly enough, Charlie was not afraid this time. He trusted Thunder. Then they entered, this time with Thunder proceeding at a dignified trot.

What a strange new sight it was for the Pigs. Even though there was a bright moon in the sky, the Forest was full of tall and deep shadows, slashes of creamy silver light, and whispery sounds. Here and there they could see someone, some*thing*, darting behind tree trunks or drifting silently from branch to branch high in the trees.

Thunder seemed to know where he was going. He maneuvered around this way and that, finally ending up in a small glade where there was an opening in the canopy of tree tops. Right in the center of the glade was a tremendous rock.

"Hold tight," he whispered to his passengers and with that warning, Thunder leapt to the top of the rock. He stood tall. This was obviously a place for Very Important Creatures.

In his deep and strong voice, the Wolfhound spoke:

"I am Thunder. My tribe of mighty Canine warriors and guardians is ten thousand years old and comes from a land far away. My tribe in **this** land is the Inventor Warriors such as you see riding on my back. Though small Creatures, they are as intelligent as the stars and as fierce as a hurricane. The Wolfhound Tribe and the Inventor Warrior Tribe always come in peace."

"We are Warriors. See? I told, you Betsy," said a small voice.

"You know my words are true. The Inventor Warriors protect me and I protect them. Always. These words are true. We welcome any who come to meet this tribe."

The mighty Dog's strong words did ring true in the deep woods. The trees themselves seemed to relax as the words of peace and protection wrapped around bark and twig, trunk and branch. Then, slowly, from the shadows there was motion.

First, a shadow appeared, then it had a sleek form, and then, hesitantly, but not in fear came a beautiful Red Fox who stepped into the moonlight. Fox had sharp ears, intelligent eyes, and a bushy tail. Two Gray Squirrels scampered almost to the ground. A Sharp-Shinned Hawk landed on a branch that hung over the glen. His eyes were black as space. Two tiny field mice appeared, very cautiously indeed, until Thunder saw them and bid them welcome. They all entered the circle of soft moonlight.

"It is our privilege to meet you," Thunder said to the small crowd. The Fliffs had climbed down and they stood in front of the Dog, between his massive paws. In unison they greeted the Animals.

"The Fliff tribe is most pleased to meet you," they said.

A careful chorus of different voices responded in mixed and soft tones. It was difficult to translate everything, but the Fliffs understood that these were good Creatures.

"I know some are shy," Thunder continued, "and they will meet us when they know us better. To you and your kind, and to all of you here, we extend a paw of friendship. This Circle of Friends will last as long as the Moon and the Sun shall guide us. So it is said."

Fred and Betsy were very impressed. They knew that Thunder was big, and no one you'd want to mess with, but because he was so gentle with them, it was easy to overlook his authority.

Now they could tell how much the Forest Creatures respected the Wolfhound. A sweet murmur seemed to fill the glade. It was as if every Creature was humming a song of contentment, and the trees and bushes passed the sound around for all to hear.

And thus went the Fliffs' first meeting in the Forest. They were impressed by the variety of Creatures and the persuasive influence of their big friend. When the tribes exchanged words of peace and friendship, the Fliffs felt a closeness with the Forest and its inhabitants.

Perhaps they would visit again. But first they would discuss a certain matter with Thunder. Two matters, in fact: Hunter and Owl. Neither of their kin had come forward.

Two weeks later, on a Friday morning, Father and Mother Fliff got a terrible scare. **Terrible!**

Father was visiting with Bert when he heard the Williams speak of going off on a skiing vacation. On no! That meant they would be put in a wire cage and taken to a boarding kennel for a week or a month or however long the Williams would be gone. No Adventures for a month? Maybe never again? It was awful! As soon as the Williams left that morning, Father gathered the family and explained what he had heard.

The reaction was immediate—Mouths open in silent cries of dismay, a plea of O..h..h... N... o..o... s, paws clasped or thrown open, eyes signaling shock and sad sorrow...

"We'll run away," Oyster squeaked. "Right now!"

"We can't do that, Silly," Rhoda said. "I think we have to talk to the Williams..."

"...as soon's they get home," Charlie shouted, standing and pointing to the ceiling like an odd statue.

"Oh sure," Sherman said. "We talk just *once* and we'll be *Show And Tell* at Chloe's school *for a month*! No thanks. I'd rather run away."

Mother held up a finely shaped paw. "Now wait, everybody. Fred, did they say *when* they're going?"

"That's just it, Betsy. Tonight! They're leaving right after dinner tonight!"

"Why haven't they packed suitcases? Or all the ski equipment? It usually takes them days to find things, never mind packing."

"Yeah, especially Chloe," Sherman snickered, making a face at his big sister, who did have a reputation for taking her time.

"Oh, well, I reckon they already did," Father said. "There's four small cases in the sewing room. They're going to go on an aeroplane. A private one, and they can't take much."

Father sat in the shavings and rubbed his forehead, as if he had a headache. "I want to run away, too," he said in a low voice. "But I can't. We can't. They'd worry about us. Or maybe go looking for us. We can't just go."

"How about leaving a message?" Charlie piped up. "Say *'Don't worry. Have a great time. See ya in a month.'* You know. Oyster could draw a Smiley Pig face. Hers. That'd make anyone laugh."

His joke didn't go over. All the Fliffs plopped onto the shavings, shaking their heads. A soft sob could be heard. Then a whisper... 'What about Thunder?'

Terrible sadness all day, but Mother and Father tried to be cheerful. They made sure that the cage was neat and clean, all the secret tools and supplies carefully hidden, and everyone's teeth properly brushed. "We'll make the best of it," she said.

No one really thought so, but they tried to be brave.

Finally, at five o'clock they heard the car drive up and the front door open and the Williams enter the house. The Fliffs could not conceal their sorrow.

They heard the family go to the Sewing Room and back downstairs.

When were they having dinner?

They heard the car start up.

What...

Footsteps. Coming up stairs. The end. A Wire cage. Doom. But, bless their brave hearts, the entire Fliff family put on smiles when they heard Chloe and Bert come over to the cage.

The Fliffs looked up. There was Bert, grinning. He had what looked like water bottles and paper bags. Then Chloe looked into the cage. She was grinning, too.

"We're going to miss you," she said. "But we brought dinner for you... it's a treat... and there's lots of extra food in the hallway. Mom and Dad said to be careful."

"See you in six days," Bert said. "Have fun." He winked.

And then they left.

The Fliffs heard the Williams lock the front door. They looked at each other in utter astonishment. Finally Father spoke.

"They... they know," he said. **"And they TRUST US! Aren't they wonderful Creatures!"**

They certainly are, everyone agreed.

That night the Inventor Warrior Clan and the Wolfhound Clan were all snug in their warm cabin on the Hill.

End.